A LOT
TO MAKE UP FOR

Books by John Buell

The Pyx

Four Days

The Shrewsdale Exit

Playground

A Lot to Make Up For

A LOT
TO MAKE UP FOR

JOHN BUELL

Farrar, Straus & Giroux
NEW YORK

Printed in the United States of America

FIRST EDITION, 1990

Design by Tere LoPrete

Library of Congress Cataloging-in-Publication Data
Buell, John.
A lot to make up for / John Buell.—1st ed.
p. cm.
I. Title.
PR9199.3.B766L68 1990 813'.54—dc20 89-25713
CIP

A LOT
TO MAKE UP FOR

1

❦

She wasn't sure she had the right street. She had left Township Street at the north end of the park and, following instructions, had gone three blocks west. There, she was to turn north on to a street called Orchard. But she could find no street signs: not on the light standard next to her, nor on the tree across the way, nor on the two fences. She hesitated for a short while, it was too cold to stand on the corner wondering, and went north as directed, walking fast to keep warm, braced against the wind, looking for number 705.

It was in the third block, on her left, a two-story house with a two-car garage. It had a large lawn unobstructed to the sidewalk and bordered by two low hedges on each side. She could barely see them in the evening darkness. It was early April, the grass would still be brown and the bushes leafless. The house lights made the dark seem deeper than it was. An ornamental "705" was lit by its own hooded light. There was no obvious doorbell. She touched a plastic strip of diffused pink light and heard gurgling chimes inside. It sounded like the new telephones. She waited. She waited until it felt like time to ring again, but still she waited. Finally she heard noises inside and the front door opened.

He was in his forties, chubby, not quite fat. He was wearing a sports shirt of different shades of green and slacks that matched the lightest shade. The clothes looked new. His hair was looped forward to cover a balding front. He didn't smile or do any of the social things. He looked at her deliberately, rudely had she been a guest, as if she were something he'd ordered; he went from her hair, auburn under a white tuque and fluttering in the wind, to her insulated jacket to her jeans to her low-cut boots.

"Oh," he said flatly, as if his curiosity had been disappointed. He caught her eye briefly, looked off somewhere past her right shoulder, and added: "What is it?"

"About your ad in the paper," she said. "I phoned earlier."

"Oh. You must have been speaking to my wife."

"Probably. It was a woman."

"Oh. Oh, yes. Then it was her. Just a moment."

He left her standing outside, the door open. It was tempting to go in, to step just inside the vestibule, but she didn't; she knew it wouldn't be well taken, you wait till they tell you. She hunched her shoulders against the wind and shifted from foot to foot. A woman finally appeared in the hall and came to the door.

She, too, was in her forties. She had dark hair, carefully done, and a sensually pretty face whose makeup looked professional. A blouse and slacks played up a long-legged athletic figure that was beginning to fill out. She also looked from tuque to boots, but without implication.

"Yes?"

"I phoned earlier. About the ad. Are you the person I was talking to?"

The woman hadn't given a name, only an address and directions.

"Yes."

She said it disdainfully as if she resented being questioned. "Come in and shut the door, it's cold."

When that was done, she said, "You're not on time, it's well after eight."

"I didn't know how long it would take to get here."

"I see. What's your name?"

She placed a slight, perhaps inadvertent, stress on "your" rather than on "name." It had a chilling effect.

"Del."

"Dell?"

"Yes."

"Is that short for something?"

"Yes, it's short for Adele."

"Oh, I see. D-E-L."

"That's right."

"You look strong enough. How old are you?"

"Twenty-three."

"That's fine. My husband says young women work harder and faster than older women, you get more for your money."

Del just looked at her.

"You said you had references."

Del gave her a sheet of notepaper on which she had written two phone numbers.

"Oh, I thought you had letters."

"Won't that do?"

"I suppose it will. I've never asked for references before, but the last two, one after the other, stole things from the TV room, things of my husband's."

Del indicated the notepaper.

"They'll tell you I don't steal things."

The woman looked at the paper as if it were some kind of puzzle. She seemed to take a long time deciding.

The chubby man in green turned into the hall quietly and suddenly, as though he'd been waiting for a cue. He looked directly into Del's eyes once and after that his eyes skipped all over her face, lips, nose, cheeks, forehead, eyebrows, throat, then hair, anywhere but back into her eyes.

As he did this, he asked: "Are you a local girl?"

"No."

"Where are you from?"

"Out west."

"Oh. Have you been in Ashton long?"

"No."

He crossed the hall, went into the other room, and

returned to stand on that side. Del would have had to turn her head to see him clearly. She kept looking at the woman, who said: "Why do you work . . . like this?"

"I have to work, like everybody else."

"I meant: at *this*, cleaning."

"Charring."

"Well, yes."

"It leaves me free."

"Free for what?"

Del didn't answer. She could sense that the man had moved into the hall a little and was looking at her.

The woman fingered the notepaper. "You do any kind of work?"

"I do normal housecleaning."

"What does that mean?"

"I do what anyone does to clean her house. But I can't move heavy furniture and I don't clean up after carpenters, for instance, or after big parties, unless I make a special deal."

"Windows?"

"On the inside. The outside if I can reach them."

"Reach them from the inside?"

"Yes."

"These you can. How much do you charge?"

"Eight-fifty an hour."

"That's a lot of money."

"For a lot of work. Hard work."

"Yes, I suppose it is. When can you come?"

"A week Friday."

"You can't come sooner?"

"No, not unless somebody cancels."

"All right. We'll see how that works out. Leave me your phone number."

She gave Del the notepaper. Del took out a ballpoint and, folding the paper to stiffen it, wrote out her first name and the number.

"It's not my number. That is, it's not my phone, it's my landlady's."

"I understand."

The woman looked at the front door to indicate that the interview was over. Del didn't move.

"May I have your name?" she asked.

"Oh. Yes, of course. I'm Mrs. Roussel, Evalynn Roussel. I run the shops."

But Del didn't know about the shops. She simply nodded and left. She didn't look back at the house. Something was telling her not to let on in any way.

When Del got home, Mrs. Poole, who had been waiting for her, was getting ready to go out. She had a Samsonite briefcase on the kitchen table and was filling it with magazines and knitting samples as she checked off a list.

"Sorry," Del said. "It took longer than I thought." She took off her tuque and jacket, and hung them over a chair. She was still puffing. "I ran most of the way home. Was Betty okay?"

"She was fine, I put her down about a half hour ago. You needn't've run on my account, they can start without me."

Mrs. Poole was a small wiry woman in her fifties.

She had a compact bony face whose every feature was sharply defined: piercing blue eyes, narrow flat eyebrows, a straight thin nose, small lips, a firm chin. Her light brown hair wasn't yet gray. She moved swiftly and spoke rapidly and seemed in a constant hurry to get things done. She was caring, nosy, and bossy.

She said: "What did she want to know, your life history?"

"Just about. She wanted letters of reference, not just phone numbers. Stuff's been stolen, twice, imagine. He wanted—"

"There was a he?"

"Oh, yes. It was his stuff that was stolen, she said. Did you have to change her?"

"Yes."

"I'm sorry, I didn't mean to—"

"That's all right. What did *he* want?"

"He asked if I was a local girl, and where was I from, and—"

"You didn't tell him."

"No. I said from out west."

"That's vague enough."

"—and then if I'd been in Ashton long. I said no."

"And?"

"Nothing. The rest of the time he just came and went."

"And her?"

"The usual things, what kind of work I do, how much I charge. She asked me why I work at cleaning. Nobody's asked me that. I said it leaves me free. Do you think she figures I want to get into people's homes or something like that?"

"No. You're young, and smart, and you don't sound illiterate. She thinks you're hard up for some reason."

"I am, in a way."

"She doesn't have to know that. Nor does he."

"She will."

The sharp blue eyes thought something over, but she said nothing about it. "How old would they be?"

"Old enough. In their forties, I'd say. She was made up. She looked nice."

"Any kids around, teenagers?"

"I didn't see any. I stayed in the vestibule."

"You mean they kept you there. Anything about his line of work?"

"No. But she runs shops of some kind. She seemed to think I should know them."

"Oh? Did she tell you the name?"

"No. Hers is Evalynn Roussel."

"Oh, yes. She uses both names for the shops. One set of stores is EvaLynn, that's high fashion, expensive, but good; the other is Roussel's, where you and I buy."

She paused, as though running through a mental checklist of questions, said, "I'll be back around 10:30," and, taking the briefcase, went out the back door to the garage.

Del took her clothes from the chair and listened for the sound of the garage door, then the car, and any sounds from upstairs, where the baby was. She liked Mrs. Poole, but she was glad to be alone from time to time. Mrs. Poole was a presence, physical and mental; it took effort to be yourself when she was around, and Del wanted to think her own thoughts and worry her own worries.

She left the kitchen and made her way to the front of the house by passing through a large dining room that had a high ceiling, real wood paneling, and two vast windows. This gave into the front hall, which continued to the back of the house and had a huge balustraded staircase leading upstairs. On the far side of this was the living room, with a bay window to the east, and, toward the back, the rooms used by Mrs. Poole.

The place was old, a hundred years if not more, and made of wood, and it creaked as Del walked across the floors and climbed the wide stairs. She lived in the two front rooms on the second floor, and had use of a third that had once been a study. The ceilings and floors had openings for stovepipes, now closed with metal caps, and square ornamental grids for hot air. The grids were handy to communicate through, and they let her hear if the baby was crying.

The baby's room was in front on the right over the dining room. She went in without trying to be noiseless, which can't be done anyway. The floor had squeaked as she came down the hall, it squeaked now, and the side of the crib rattled as she leaned over it. The baby didn't stir. She was just over a year old, still small for her age, slowly catching up to normal. Del gently pried the milk bottle from her hand and tried to replace it with a similar bottle of water. But the baby's hand stayed limp. Del placed the water within reach.

On a makeshift changing table, a backless dresser with a pad and a sheet of plastic, was the diaper Mrs. Poole had changed. Del used the old-fashioned kind at home, it was cheaper, and the disposables when she took the baby with her. She carried the diaper to the second-floor bathroom at the back of the house, rinsed it in the toilet bowl, and put it in a covered diaper pail where others like it were soaking. Mrs. Poole had changed the baby; Del did all the rest. She took the pail downstairs to the basement and dumped it in the clothes washer and got it going for a pre-wash rinse. As she went back up the stairs, she heard the phone ringing. She took it in the kitchen, on a wall phone near the hall.

"Hello."

"Is this where Del lives?"

"Yes. I'm Del."

"I didn't recognize you, I expected someone else to answer. This is Evalynn Roussel."

"Oh, yes. What—?"

"I've rechecked my schedule, a week Friday is simply impossible, you'll have to come sooner, I'm having people in. When can you come?"

"I'm sorry, I can't. That Friday's the only time. I'm booked right up till then."

"Surely you can make time. Do you work at night?"

"No."

"You must have days off, how about then?"

"I'm sorry, no. I have things to take care of at . . . here."

"Can't that wait? I need someone desperately. My husband says the place is filthy. I'll pay you overtime."

"No, I can't."

"Double time, then."

"No, Mrs. Roussel, I have commitments. I'm sorry."

"Oh God, what'll I do?"

"How about your other cleaners?"

"No, no, no, no. That's finished."

"Do you still want me to come a week Friday?"

"Yes, yes, don't cancel that, whatever you do."

She hung up, as easily as looking somewhere else. Del put the phone back slowly.

She couldn't get used to being treated like the help, she resented it every time it happened, and that was sooner or later with every customer. She wasn't experienced enough to expect it. She kept the price high on Mrs. Poole's advice: charge the limit, they find less for you to do. That didn't change any attitudes, it only made the help expensive.

She worked Tuesdays and Thursdays for Mrs. Poole, keeping the big house clean. That took care of the rent and gave her the run of the house, within limits. It wasn't home, nothing would ever be, but it worked: she was able to take care of her child, to pay her way, to keep busy. That was important, especially for her. She'd been on drugs until before the baby was born.

She was on her own now, away from those who had helped her, and she had told no one. No one could understand, except from the inside. What was hers to know, she knew from bitter experience: she was an addict, forever, always recovering, always at risk, accepting everything that came her way, trying to resent nothing, or at least not for long. She didn't have to be motivated, all she had to do was remember: the violence that was as certain as the ecstasies and lasted much longer, the agonies coming out of it, trying to do it before term, the baby's withdrawal pains, a tiny screaming little person who hadn't deserved anything but love and care, and got her. The guilt of it made her cringe. That, too, had to be accepted, and let go. But it always came back. She had no dreams for the future, it was all she could do to live in the present.

She heard the rinse coming to an end and she went back to the basement to set the regular wash cycle.

It was raining, and had been for two days. The dirt roads were still thawing, and the rain had turned them into puddles and mush and holes hidden by the water. The trick was to guess which puddles had the potholes. He wasn't doing very well at that, but he was moving and, in a complex way, not disliking the difficulties. He'd done it for years and he was too old to be upset by natural occurrences. He didn't mind going slow, it suited him, he was in his late sixties. And it suited the truck; it was an eight-year-old Ford pickup, battered by the previous owner, restored somewhat by him, and it ran well, under certain conditions.

He kept it in second, not to have to brake all the time, and went largely by feel; at the least skid he eased off the gas. He watched for puddles and tried to straddle them, but what he really looked at was the countryside. Each year, each season, it differed, never the same, never to repeat. Right now, April, it was brown, every shade of it: the light, almost yellow stubble in the fields, the dark leafless trees, the ditches where no ice had formed overnight, the thousands of grayish fence posts, old rusted wire, the hills he could make out a little, and, of course, the road. The greens looked smug, he thought, for having borne the winter, cedar bush, hemlocks among the bare maples, pines. There were still heaps of snow to show them up. In less than a month they wouldn't stand out anymore, everything would be every shade of green.

A sign said he would soon be going downhill, but he really didn't see it. He was already braking a little, then more, and he put the truck in first. It slid in the mud, held, slid again, and sank and swerved in the soft spots, nothing serious, just spring driving. In a while the dirt road ended at a paved highway. He took that, to his left. And soon another sign, which he didn't have to see, announced: ASHTON.

The highway became one of the town's streets. He turned right at a traffic light, went a while, and turned again, left this time, into a street called City Gardens, along which there really were small parks. Facing one of these was a hardware store called Foster's. He parked in front of it and took a small V-belt from the seat next to him. It used to run his water pump, it needed replacing. On a rainy day you do indoor jobs.

"Hello, Martin," said the man behind the counter.

"Bernie. It's a sloppy day."

"That's what everybody's saying. A guy just came in from . . ."

But Martin Lacey wasn't listening. Something was interfering, inside—encircling pain, jolting the air out of him, fast, sudden, sustained, like a blow that wasn't going to end. He held on to the counter with both hands, weak now and getting weaker, the pain increasing, and he slipped to one knee, then the other. Things were beginning to disappear.

"Bernie . . ."

He barely whispered it before falling into nothingness.

He was gazing at a dim whiteness that seemed flat and shapeless. He couldn't tell what it was, but he was sure it was real and not something he was imagining. He waited and wondered, and let his eyes wander from far to overhead where the whiteness was stronger, glaring at first, and suddenly he understood. He was looking at a ceiling and he was in a bed. It had a side of stainless tubing like a gate. And another. A hospital bed.

In the instant he felt terror, which faded quickly, for nothing visible was threatening him, then fear, sharp and subtle, which he knew he'd have to face as often as it arose. And that, too, subsided as he became more aware of things.

A narrow plastic tube, taped to the outside of his right hand, went to a plastic bag on a stand. The bag had printing on it: clean, assertive letters, like an ad. Several wires went from his chest to a machine which he could have seen by sitting up and turning his head. He didn't try. There were other beds, one on each side at least, as far as he could tell, occupied by men rigged with tubes and wires. The glare, which made the ceiling visible, turned out to be hooded work lights near the beds, dim really, but to him quite bright. There seemed to be no windows, no time of day. He didn't have his watch. He was unshaved, by two or three days.

His chest felt as if somebody had jumped on it. He began to remember.

"Well, Mr. Lacey," she said, "it's nice to have you back."

She was cheerful without being oppressive about it, brisk, about thirty. He hadn't heard her come in, and thought he should have, and that bothered him, like a puzzle he didn't want to do. He noticed the genuine smile in her eyes and, for no reason, the fineness of her brown hair.

"How do you feel?" she asked.

"Not bad, I guess. I haven't tried anything yet. My chest hurts."

"It should. They worked on you for a while."

"I had a heart attack, didn't I?"

"That's right."

"I feel funny."

"How, funny?"

Talking was exhausting him. He felt as if he were pushing words out of himself and uphill. But his head stayed clear, distant.

"Strange. Far away. I could be someone else."

"It's probably the drugs. It'll wear off. You'll feel different in the morning."

"Then it's night."

"It is that, three . . . fifteen. If you need anything, here's your cord."

"Thanks."

She left as noiselessly as she had entered. He lifted his head a little to see where the door was. A small thing, and it hurt to do it. But it was better than not knowing. There was no door, it was a permanent opening, so they could glide in and out, and hear you if things went wrong.

With that settled, he glanced as well as he could at the patients on each side of him, but saw little of them except the tubes and stands and guardrails. The far ceiling was the easiest thing to look at. It was like nothing. But nothing won't do.

He remembered that it was night and felt its timelessness, and his thoughts were random and insistent because he didn't have the energy to control them, and that let fear come up like an urgent agenda he couldn't attend to. What's next can't be good. Down the road is just that, down. Fear never has doubts. The perfect liar. Why is it so much easier to believe the worst? Because the worst is what can happen, that's why. Another one of Murphy's laws. Get off it. Fear leads nowhere. Yeah, well, what leads where? What *is* the worst?

In two days he was out of intensive care and into a large room or small ward with three other men, younger than he, two beds on each long side, and with four television sets suspended from the ceiling more or less in line with each bed. The sets had control devices, for rent, that plugged in near each bed. He didn't get one. The place was noisy, three sets on all the time. There were two phones, one for each pair of beds, and a lot of traffic: cleaners, orderlies, nurses, a woman chaplain, the girls in dietetics, doctors, interns, medical students, volunteers, visitors. It was almost a shock, but he welcomed it.

A young resident, efficient and full of knowledge, with stylish hair and a well-formed mustache, took his history and asked a lot of intelligent questions and nodded at the answers and made notes of everything on a clipboard. He offered no opinion.

An authoritative woman in her forties, tall and firm, probably the head nurse, asked about his circumstances.

"Can you get time off work? Will that be a problem?"

"No. I don't work for anybody."

"You're unemployed."

"You could say that. Nobody employs me."

"Do you find that difficult to accept?"

"Well, no. I think it's great."

"You're retired?"

"In a way. I do a little farming, of sorts."

"Isn't that heavy work?"

"Sometimes it is."

"Is there any way to avoid that heavy work?"

"I always try to avoid it."

"You know what I mean."

"Sure. I'll have to see."

"What about at home?"

"Home?"

"I understand you live alone."

"You must have access to my income tax returns."

She finally smiled at that.

"No," she said, "friends of yours, a Mr. Phil Baines

and his wife, were in, the first night you were here. We asked him a few questions."

"Yes, I live alone. That's no problem either."

"Well, the doctor will explain things to you."

An orderly wheeled him to other floors and different departments for testing. In cardiology he saw his heartbeat as blips on a TV monitor. More young doctors conducted interviews. Later a pleasant girl explained the meal system and left cards for him to tick off his choices. It was bustling, and tiring. Two of the men had afternoon visitors. The TV stayed on, and a radio for the early-season baseball games. He struggled with the toilet equipment and prevailed. Busy, too busy to think, a good thing perhaps, but fear kept trying to butt in. There was no coming to yourself in an organized rush.

Supper was early, and awkward and messy in bed. The other men seemed to have evolved a technique, it takes time to get good at it. Time. The men exchanged a few remarks, the rough civilities of having to be together, but no one imposed conversation on anybody. The TV news, followed by the sitcoms. Then a visitor.

It was Phil Baines. He looked round the room to find the right bed. He was tall, but built so much like a wrestler that he looked squat, in his sixties, with short gray hair, lines in his face, and clear gray-blue eyes. He was dressed for outside, a wool shirt, a down-filled jacket. He was very welcome.

"Well," he said, "how are you?" And he meant it.

"I'm all right."

"They tell you what you got? I mean, to explain the heart attack."

"Not exactly. The tests seem pretty normal."

"They say that or you say that?"

"A little of both. When all the tests are in, the man in charge will tell me."

"You sure look better off than you did three nights ago. We dropped in, Marge and I, to see how things were."

"Yeah, I heard."

"I said I'd do for next of kin. No point trying to reach people, it'd be just bad news with no knowing what."

"I'll phone them when I get home."

"We got your keys the other night. Your pickup's at my place."

"Yeah, thanks." He knew without asking that Marge would take care of things at his house.

"Bernie phoned us, just after they took you away."

"He must've called the ambulance."

"Yeah, right off."

They talked a while longer, and Phil stood up and put a paper bag on the bed.

"Shaving things," he said. "No point in wearing you down. I'll come in when I can." He took down the number on the phone, saying, "I'll get Marge to call you," and he left.

He began to think of home, such as it was, things that needed doing. And new problems.

The following afternoon a Dr. Benoit, a man in his fifties, explained to him that he was recovering well, that they didn't know what had caused the incident but something was putting a strain on his heart and they'd do more testing to see if anything revealed itself. The next day two encouraging nurses got him to his feet and walked with him and gave him a routine to follow. It was a relief to go to a real john, to shave properly and wash and do the things you do when you're on two feet. Soon.

Stan Hagan was driving slowly through East Windsor. He was doing twenty at most, not wanting the special alertness that went with speed. Even thirty can be fast if you want to keep your head quiet. He was in no hurry, and it would save on gas, and it let him look and think, if he wanted to. He knew where he was going and what he expected, which didn't amount to much, and time was unimportant.

He was in a six-year-old Dodge wagon which he kept free of complaints, except age. He was leaving East Windsor to go to the next town. He'd be jobless for a time, and if for long, he'd be broke. Then he'd find work again, at more odd jobs. The wagon gave him an edge there. He didn't worry, he'd been doing it for quite a while, and it suited his present purposes. If he kept on the move, at the right times, he was just a guy going from job to job; but if he stayed too long at low-level work, he was a help-out, a failure. He was twenty-seven years old. But a lot of people seemed to be out of work, so he wasn't that conspicuous.

Near the edge of town he stopped for the complicated lights at the throughway, crossed it, stayed on the two-lane secondary, and gradually brought the car to an easily controlled forty-five. It was hilly country. The road climbed and dipped in long stretches and curved and kept revealing more hills. There was no one in front or behind. The sun was somewhere over his right shoulder and climbing, the hollows were still in shadow. Some maples had sap buckets on them, and the porous crystalline snow was ready for another day of melting. The season was growing warmer day by day. You could almost stop and watch it. It's all there, he said to himself, not quite knowing what he meant, but only that he did mean it. Clear and clean and real.

Soon in the distance was the packed geometric look of the town, an overcast of smoke, and along the road a reception hall, unfarmed lots, a mechanic's repair shop with rusty machinery outside, an old house with a placard on the veranda announcing antiques. No work there.

The highway sign said ASHTON, and five hundred feet later the fancier town sign repeated it and added, *30 mph.* He went very slow again, looking at things. There was a quarry of some sort on his left with two big trucks waiting to be loaded, on his right a rail line that arrived at discolored freight sheds and later at an old-fashioned station that looked like a tourist attraction. Past these was a small factory with tacked-on additions and piles of clean lumber, a feed-and-grain cooperative, a farm-equipment dealer, a still-closed vegetable outlet, and near it an ice-cream stand waiting for summer, then at an intersection two catercorner gas stations with big lots and a traffic light hanging over the middle of the highway.

Past the light, the stores and businesses went on for a few blocks, some spreading into the side streets, and abruptly there were old three-story houses with wide lawns and tall trees, and these gave way to newer places with less ground, and still farther a few mobile homes on small lots, followed by fields and farmland and a speed-limit sign that told him he was well out of town. He turned in at the first driveway, backed around, and went back to town. Things were quiet; it was a little past nine on a Monday morning.

He returned to the traffic light and turned left. He was on another main street: a few houses quite old and close to the street, a clinic, two churches almost facing each other, an old hotel, shops, the city hall with monumental writing above big doors, and a little farther the post office, a small four-square cement-and-glass building with flags flying. He parked in its lot and went in.

There was no one around. He gawked at the notices and posters, no hurry, no clamoring for service, this wasn't megalopolis, all low profile here. Eventually a woman in her thirties, who must have heard him walking around, came in from the back and stood behind the counter. She had voluminous black hair, a bright red blouse, and small features exaggerated by big tinted glasses.

"Good morning," she said.

"Nice day." And he went into it. "A while back I sent a general-delivery letter here. To Adele Symons, S-y-m-o-n-s. I wonder if she picked it up."

The clerk crossed the floor behind the counter and from a slot in a rack of boxes took out a small bundle of letters, flipped through them, stopped at one, and put them all back.

"No," she said, "it's still here."

"Oh. I thought she might be in Ashton."

"I guess she isn't," she said, leaning forward on the counter as if inviting confidences.

He sensed it vaguely, a feeling that he could have continued the conversation, but it would have led nowhere he wanted to go.

"Right. I'll try again sometime. Thanks a lot."

He took the car from the parking lot, left it on the first side street he came to, and walked along the main street until he found a likely store, one with magazines on display. There he bought a regional paper, *The Hampton Journal*, and another, smaller publication called *The Bulletin Board* that contained only want ads, notices, calling-card advertising, week-by-week sales, and anything that could be typed in a few lines. In the car he searched the papers for rooms to let in Ashton. *The Bulletin Board* yielded five, only one with "cooking," no prices.

On foot once more and on the same street he found a supermarket, part of a nationwide chain, and on the wall between the two sets of automatic glass doors he checked through the handmade notices. Two possibles, one on Grove, the other on Mill Street.

He asked directions of an old man who had come in with a little girl and who was waiting, seated near the entrance, as if time had no meaning. The directions were orderly, consider this street as a baseline, he oriented his newspaper, he sounded like a retired surveyor.

"Place to live?" he said.

"Yes."

"Looking for work?"

"Yeah. Is that your granddaughter?"

"My great-granddaughter. I'm eighty-two."

The two men grinned at each other and all but laughed out loud.

The street the supermarket was on, Township Street, maybe it really was a baseline, formed a T with another town-long street, City Gardens. Left for some six blocks was Grove, right on Grove, to a house with a sagging veranda and in such disrepair that he drove on by, made a U-turn at the first corner, got back on City Gardens, and went back across town to Mill Street.

Here it was different. The fences and hedges were well kept, the lawns free of junk except for the spring snow and winter debris, the houses in good repair. The address he stopped at was a two-story house, three if they'd converted the attic, with a deep lawn and two big maples, one at each end of the frontage. The house had been extended in the rear, the veranda along with it, and a paved driveway led past all this to what looked like a garage and workshop, heated, it seemed, for there was a metal chimney on the roof. He went up to the side entrance and pressed the buzzer.

A tall woman, middle-aged, wearing men's work clothes, opened the inside door and unlatched the aluminum door for him to pull open. She had a lean, handsome face, no makeup, lines where a drawing would have them, glasses, and cared-for hair that was all brown. The work clothes made her look strong. She didn't smile.

"What is it?"

"I saw your notice at the supermarket, about a room."

"Well?"

"Well, if it's available, I'd like to look at it."

"It's available. First off, though, you got references of any kind?"

"I've been staying in East Windsor, I can give you that phone number."

"You were working there?"

"Yeah, I was."

"You can gimme that number, too."

"All right."

He knew what the next question was going to be.

"You working in Ashton?" she said.

"Not yet. I just got here. I got a little money saved."

"You're alone?"

"Yeah."

She led the way along the veranda to the third, and last, door and they went in. It was more than the usual room. It had a compact electric stove, the kind that takes 220 wiring, a small fridge standing on some sort of cupboard, a sink under one window, a hinged table under the other, and a toilet with a shower stall about the size of a coffin. It was a basic do-it-yourself job with secondhand materials, probably from an auction. It even had an old TV set, color, with a radio in it.

"It's nice," he said, "but I expected, you know, just a room."

"That's what they all say. The price is the same as any good room in town. My husband built this. A mini-motel he called it, keeps people out of your house. It's long been paid for."

"He's a good worker."

"Was. He's gone now. You gonna take it?"

"What are you charging?"

"You keep it clean, forty a week, you don't, fifty, and I'll be the judge of if it's clean."

"All right. I'll keep it clean."

"You pay in advance, on Fridays. This week's short, so gimme thirty."

He paid her and she gave him a key and left.

He backed the wagon to his door and unloaded his luggage. There wasn't much, a plastic suit container, a side-opening duffel bag, a canvas tote bag, all under a tarp in the back of the car. He didn't want the luggage to be visible in the wagon. It would say he was on the move, not as a tourist, or a man in some kind of business—the wagon and the luggage were too run-down for that—no, just not a resident, not living anywhere, another stranger, drifting, with city written all over him, no roots, no loyalties, nobody to know, no one to know him, the ideal of the twentieth century, alone, god-like, a joke in the universe, about as self-sufficient as a bug without a plant to chew on.

He called a halt to that line of thought, he could sense it as subtly hidden self-pity. They'd warned him about that. He had another call to make.

* * *

He got back on Township Street and found the city-hall building he had passed earlier. It was a likely place to look. He turned into the parking area, pulled up where the sign said VISITORS, and as he was getting out of the wagon saw another sign, POLICE, over a much-used side door. There it was, he didn't have to look any farther. He'd learned you don't go around a small town asking people where the police station is, not if you're going to stay there for a while asking questions of your own, it sets up too much curiosity on the town's grapevine. And he'd also learned that if you're going to check out a town systematically, you better let the police in on it, or they'll hear about you and get very suspicious and keep at you until they're satisfied you're up to no harm. No resentment. That's just the way it has to go. Strangers are strangers. For that reason he was dressed respectably, slacks, jacket, sports shirt, under a short parka-like winter coat. He went in.

He came almost immediately to a long, solid counter behind which was a lot of floor space, with four desks, two on each side, facing the middle of the office, and on the far wall a row of filing cabinets where a young uniformed policeman was doing paperwork. A radio was on at a phone-in show. To the left a woman in her forties, in a white blouse and cardigan, sat at a typing desk that was part of the counter. Beside her, forming the corner, was a phone console, radio equipment, a computer terminal, and the top half of that wall was glass, through which he could see another office. The woman saw him and said, "Good morning."

"Morning," he said. "I'd like to talk to the chief."

She spoke into the phone, barely audible over the radio show, and said to him, "That way"—to his left—"the first door."

It was the office he had seen through the glass partition. A man who seemed to be in his fifties was seated at a large table that had been shoved against the back wall under maps of the area and the town. He was in civvies, a suit, not new, with necktie; he had short gray hair, glasses, a long thin face and blue eyes that gave the impression of cheerfulness. He didn't get up, he simply swiveled around and waved to the mate's chair at the other end of the table.

"Have a seat."

"Thanks."

"What can I do for you?"

"Probably not very much, but I want to explain what I'm doing."

From his wallet he took out the driver's license and registration and handed them to the chief.

"My name is Hagan, Stan Hagan."

"Hagan. I've never seen that one. Usually it's O'Hagan." He handed the things back. "Tell me, Stan, are we going to be talking about something legal or criminal?"

"No. Just human."

"All right."

"I'm trying to find somebody, a girl, a woman. Adele Symons. She'd be twenty-three, twenty-four now."

"You're not an investigator of some kind, bill collector?"

"No. I'm on my own."

"You a relative?"

"No. I know her, I'm . . . a friend, I guess."

"Are you trying to report a missing person?"

"Not really. She's not missing, except to me."

"Yeah, that's a way of looking at it. You realize that officially there's nothing I can do. I can't even ask *you* questions."

"I know that."

"And even if I knew of this young lady, which I don't, I wouldn't tell you anything without knowing a whole lot more."

"I know that, too."

"All right, we got that straight. Now, what are you telling me?"

"Well, I'm looking for her, and I'm going to keep looking for her, and that means I'm going to be looking all over town, and I thought you should know it."

The chief sat back and looked at Stan and said nothing for a long time. It was almost embarrassing. But Stan was used to silence, and it wasn't the right moment to leave. The chief's look wasn't hostile, or even suspicious; it was as if he were considering things, experience trying to arrive at a judgment.

"What makes you think she's in Ashton?"

"Nothing definite. It's just a possibility."

"You must have something to go on."

"Yeah, but it's not much. A Christmas card. She sent one to her sister last December. There was no return address. The postmark was Middleton. So I started there. I found nothing. Then over to East Windsor. Now I'm here in Ashton."

"Is she married?"

"Her sister didn't think so."

"Living with somebody?"

"I don't know."

"You're not actually any of my business, Stan, not as a cop. Oh, I know, once you get looking around, some of my men are going to hear about you and all that, but that won't make it a police matter. Still, you've been over at Middleton, then East Windsor, now here, and I can't help wondering why you're doing it—not as a cop, you understand."

"She was part of my life sometime back. More than part. There's a lot I have to make up for."

"Yeah. You been working?"

"Off and on, enough to keep going."

"Do you happen to have any references?"

"Yes, phone numbers. And this."

From an envelope he took a note and passed it over. The chief read, "To Anybody, I can give this man a good OK, just call me. Maurice Plante, manager, Metro Stores, Middleton." He nodded and gave it back.

"You staying in town?"

"I got a room on Mill Street, 95 Mill Street."

"Oh yeah. I hope things work out for you. Let me know, eh?"

"I will."

He went round to the front of the building and up the stairs to the city-hall offices and after a few inquiries he bought a map of the town.

2

❦

On Friday the baby was awake early, before six, and Del was able to be out of the house by seven. She had organized what she could the night before: the pop-open cans of baby food, a spoon, the disposable diapers, a bag for garbage, a towel and washcloth and a plastic changing pad that could also serve as something to play on, a stuffed knitted creature she had made that Betty loved, a noise-making lamb, an extra pacifier. In the morning she had only to prepare three baby bottles of milk and pack them in a cooler bag. She put all this, including the baby, into a secondhand stroller that could be folded out to double as a carriage.

She walked to Orchard Street and got to Roussel's a little after 7:30.

Evalynn Roussel answered the door and stood there,

visibly disappointed, looking at Del and at the child in the stroller. Finally she said: "Well?"

Del, not knowing what this meant, replied, "Well, I'm here, this is the Friday we agreed on."

"You're here to work?"

"Well, yes. There's no other reason."

"I thought that—with the baby"—she jerked her head at the child—"you were here to tell me you couldn't work."

"I would've phoned."

"Yes, of course, I should have realized. Come in."

Inside, Del took off her jacket and the baby's snowsuit and, not invited to use the vestibule closet, put them on the floor against the closet door.

"Can you work with—with the baby to take care of?"

"Oh yes."

"Do you always do that? I mean take the baby with you?"

"Yes."

"Can't you get a sitter?"

"No."

"Isn't there a day care you could use?"

"No. It's expensive. And I don't want to."

"You won't be working *all* the time. You'll have to spend *some* time with the baby. I can't pay you for that."

"I'm not asking you to. If I have to spend time with her, I deduct it from the total, that's all."

"Very well."

She waited impatiently while Del set things up on

the floor of the handiest room, the dining room: first the changing pad, then the baby, then the creature and the lamb for her to play with. The rest she left in the stroller and wheeled it into the room to keep it from blocking the hall.

She noticed Mr. Roussel on the stairs, watching this, in suit and tie, looking as though he was surprised, but before she could even look at him, he was down the stairs and gone to the back of the house. Soon after that, she heard the steady rumble of the garage door opening electrically, then closing, but she didn't know what it was.

Mrs. Roussel had a handwritten list on a clipboard. She showed Del where the cleaning supplies were—some in the basement, some in a spare room on the first floor, more in a closed-off space in the garage. In each room she specified the time to be spent on it, one hour for the kitchen, a half hour each for the two main bathrooms, fifteen minutes for the one in the basement, a half hour for the living room, the same for the bedroom. One wall of the living room was organized for entertainment: receiver, amplifier, speakers, compact-disc player, TV, VCR, a camcorder, racks of tapes and movies.

"I don't want the baby in here at all," said Mrs. Roussel. "You're not to clean any of this"—she made an inclusive gesture with both hands to take in the equipment—"or use it. You can use the radio in the kitchen."

When the tour was over, she put the clipboard on the kitchen table.

"I'll leave this so you can refer to it. It would be handy if you ticked off what you do, but I won't insist on it, all right? Do you have any questions?"

"No," Del said.

"I'll be in from time to time whenever I can."

In a short while Del again heard the even rumble of the garage door, and this time she looked out the window and saw a car backing to the street and heard the door as it rolled shut.

She began with the upstairs. She brought up what she needed in two trips, the vacuum cleaner with attachments, a plastic bucket, a squeegee mop, large sponges, cloths, detergent, spray-on cleaner, scouring powder, rubber gloves. She tucked her own gloves in her back pockets, one in each, dangling, she'd use them when the others got too damp. She did the silent work with one ear out for the baby. She dusted all surfaces, lifting every object and replacing it slightly differently and in a clear order so that she'd know she'd been there.

During the noisy work, vacuuming and running the taps, she stopped from time to time to listen for the baby's noises. During one of these pauses, she thought she heard the garage door and expected to see Mrs. Roussel. But nothing happened and she forgot about it. She did the main bedroom, a guest room, a sort of sitting room with a TV set in it, a workroom with all kinds of women's clothing hanging on racks, probably from the shops, the bathrooms, one off the main bedroom, one off the hall. When she was bringing things back downstairs, she heard the garage door, unmistakable this time, once, twice, for opening and closing, and waited for Mrs. Roussel to come in. But Mrs. Roussel didn't come in.

Del went upstairs slowly to get the rest of the cleaning things, still listening, and on her way down she realized that the sounds she'd heard meant that the car was leaving, not arriving. She must have missed the arrival. Maybe it arrived the very first time when she thought she'd heard something. It didn't matter. It was none of her business what people did in their own homes. It was 11:30, time to fix lunch and prepare the baby's food.

When she had things warming on the kitchen stove, she thought again of what she'd heard and decided to take a look. From the kitchen she went into a short hall that led to a back door, to the basement, and to the connecting door for the garage. She looked in.

There was a pale blue car on the near side. Two cars must have left around eight o'clock, first his, then hers. She had seen hers leave. One had come back. She didn't know which one. Maybe they were checking up on her, to see how she was working, or to see if she was stealing. But that didn't make sense, you can't tell just by looking.

It was still none of her business. She returned to the kitchen, a little on the alert, and, using the stroller as a high-chair, she fed the baby.

It began to be her business sometime after two o'clock.

She had done the front hall, the dining room, the back hall, the living room, and she was planning to do the kitchen last. She had been very careful in the living room. She had dusted things delicately, got into corners and under the furniture where she could, and had avoided the designated wall units. She didn't even touch the fancy little spotlights on the black floor-to-ceiling poles. She put the vacuum cleaner back in the spare room and was on her way to the kitchen to take a break. Something in the living room caught her eye. In the instant she thought the baby might have crawled into the forbidden area. She stopped and turned and took a look.

He was standing in the middle of the room. He had on a short light dressing gown that came to just above his knees. He was barefoot. He looked smug and serious despite the seeming slight smile that appeared when he spoke.

"I've been watching you," he said. "I hope you don't mind."

She couldn't move. She quickly made sure she knew where the baby was, on her pad on the floor of the front hall. The stroller was still in the kitchen with the baby's stuff in it. Beyond that, she couldn't think.

"Those gloves hanging out of your back pockets are—great."

He sounded as if he were congratulating her for having thought of it, as though she'd planned it.

Del found her thoughts and her voice. She knew she had to stall him.

"Mrs. Roussel said she'd come back, she might be here any second."

"No. She won't. I told her I'd look in."

"I'll tell her about this."

"About what? She won't believe you."

Del edged her way toward the front hall.

"You won't have to do much," he said, "just hold it"—he flung off the dressing gown—"in your hand."

He seemed to think this should fascinate her. Del couldn't believe it. But it gave her a chance to get to the baby. She wrapped her in the pad and managed to put her in the stroller. As calmly and deliberately as she could, she converted the stroller into a carriage and she pushed it into the hall.

"We could give the baby something to keep her quiet."

"No!"

He pressed a switch near the wall units and the spotlights came on.

"All I want to do is tape it. It's got special makeup. I'll give you a hundred dollars."

"No."

"Two hundred, then."

"There are people who do that stuff, get them."

"I need someone new. It's no good unless it's someone new. It'd be better if you undressed."

Del got her jacket and the baby's snowsuit from the vestibule floor and put them over the baby in the carriage.

"If you go, I'll spread the word on you, you won't be able to work, ever."

Del got to the front door, opened it, turned and pulled the carriage outside front-end first.

"Ever! Ever!"

She quickly got behind the carriage and ran some

distance before she stopped to put on her jacket. The baby was crying. Del took time to put her in her snowsuit and give her one of the bottles.

Then she walked, shaking, trying not to be afraid, not crying, not yet.

Common sense told her that he couldn't come after her, not right away, not until he took time to get dressed, but fear said he could do that quickly and then use the car to track her down. Running was no use, not with the stroller, it would only make her stand out and it would keep upsetting the baby. She walked as fast as she could to Township Street, figuring by now he'd be doing something, crossed it and headed south, facing the oncoming traffic. That way he couldn't pull up behind her, and if he made a U-turn and faced her, she could run past him and disappear before he could turn again.

She didn't feel absurd doing it, it was very practical, a decision, and she was in control of herself, no panic. But she was close to it. Her fear was real and it was about something real, and she couldn't stop it by just deciding to. It was a terror born of experience. She expected anger, fury, an explosion of hatred. She had seen it once before, the rage that can go with sex. It was inexplicable, sudden, murderous; it had made her run from someone she had loved, and the very thought of it could still crush her. She had seen him at his worst, and hers, and they blamed each other, he more than she, for his was the violence.

It had been there all along, growing, waiting to burst

out, a burning resentment of the very pleasures they were pursuing. What had once been choice was now habit and need, pleasures now joyless that they couldn't stop pursuing. The less the return, the stronger the pursuit, the greater the misery. It was always worse *after*, after the sex, after the days of booze, after the ecstasy of cocaine, something still hungry, and still empty, and even more demanding, the letdown that told you you'd never be happy, but that you'd try again, and again, addicted to pleasures that now mocked you. I was that for him, he was that for me, and he raged and screamed against it, hating his body and my body and the very joys that gave him nothing but misery.

"You! Goddam it, you!" He spit out the words, hardly able to speak without hissing. "You're not doing anything for me—just a come-on! And nothing! Nothing!"

"It's not *me*!"

"It is you! You're there, there! Don't you know what you're doing?"

"It's not my fault."

"It's *not mine*!"

The words were lost in the bitter yelling but not in the remembering. They were held fast in the shock of being hit, the sudden impact of a fist to the cheek, the dizziness, the jolt of being hurled against the wall, the sound of him furiously destroying the room as she crawled out and onto the street and finally away.

She was pregnant then, and didn't know it, and alone. By the time she did know, she was in her third month. She hadn't felt much movement, the drugs were covering up a lot of it, and she hadn't wondered about the missed periods, but she sensed the changes in her body and went to a clinic and found out. It was then she knew she was doing something awful to the little life within her and tried, and tried again and again, to stop but simply couldn't. She cut down because she didn't have the money to buy all she wanted. She had to work at low-pay jobs, part-time and at odd times, and it got less and less until she had nothing at all. In her fifth month, broke and exhausted and worried about her baby, she heard of a shelter connected with the clinic and went there.

It was the baby that motivated her to enter the ordeal of going off drugs, that and the desire to be clean, and it was someone she met at the clinic, Elizabeth Stevens, a nurse who belonged to a religious order, who helped her get through the worst of it. The baby was born a month early, small for its time, tense as if its body were all cramps, hurting beyond its own capacity to yell. Her own pain she could endure, she had brought that on herself, but the baby's suffering was innocent, and it had been caused by her. The guilt of it overwhelmed her. All she could do was hold her screaming baby day after day and weep and weep, the lowest point in her life.

She called her Elizabeth after Sister Elizabeth, then Betty, then all sorts of other endearing nicknames as things improved. The baby absorbed her fully, a baby, she knew, who was already an addict, and her grief and shock became a grim determination to protect her infant. Elizabeth found her a place to stay, and when she was strong enough to travel and to look for work,

Elizabeth used her network of connections to have her move from Toronto to Montreal and finally to Ashton, where sisters of another religious order were able to help her start living on her own. She longed to go back there, to visit, to hear them singing their office, as they called it, but she denied herself that. She wasn't ready for the past. Only for the hard present. It had gone fairly well until now, except for the strange man who offered to drug her baby so he could have his kind of sex undisturbed.

The Poole house, number 18 on Station Street, was built on a slope. It was well away from the street, three old-fashioned stories and an attic, with a veranda on three sides, some of it screened off. It looked out on the railroad station, now used only for freight, and on a whole block of partly paved yard. It was reached by a walk of three terraced levels and stone steps and by an asphalt driveway that went up the slope and around the back of the house. When she got there, Del had to pause on the sidewalk to rest a little. She was too close to home to be afraid, but she was still agitated, and now that she was here she felt how tired she was. She put one prolonged indignant effort into getting the carriage up the long slope and around to the kitchen door. The door was locked. Mrs. Poole wasn't home yet.

She let herself in and kept busy. She hung up their clothes and brought all the baby stuff upstairs. She was deliberately avoiding dwelling on things and feeling sorry for herself, the sort of mood that leads to justifying a drink or a pill. She changed the baby and put the disposables in a plastic bag and into the garbage along with the discards from lunchtime. Downstairs, she put the baby in the playpen. She washed the baby bottles and refilled them and put them in the fridge.

None of that did any good. She kept remembering, and the event kept replaying itself, and she was beginning to get bitterly angry. She decided not to mention it to anyone. Somehow it seemed shameful, something to hide, as if she were guilty in some way. She sensed that her anger was turning in on her. That didn't make sense, she had no reason to be angry with herself. That's the sort of thing *he*'d want her to feel. She made tea and wondered what to do next. And Mrs. Poole drove up.

She left her car by the kitchen, tried the door, and walked in. She had a big bulging purse hanging from one shoulder and she was carrying a shopping bag full of cones of yarn. It was nearly 3:30. She looked at Del and knew something was wrong.

"The baby all right?"

"Oh yes, she's fine."

"You're a little early, aren't you?"

"A bit, I left sooner than I expected."

"Oh."

She hesitated, evidently deciding not to question Del any further, and took her things to her workroom.

Del was feeling the stress of avoiding the subject, of having to pretend things were all right, of almost lying about it. That could only get worse, and more complicated, because the thing wasn't over yet. Reluctantly she took out the phone book and looked up the

EvaLynn shops. Mrs. Roussel wasn't in at the first number. She tried a second, was given a third number, and finally she was saying: "Mrs. Roussel, this is Del. I'm sorry to call you at work . . ."

"Wait a minute. Who?"

"Del." She felt her heart slipping to the floor. "Del, the girl cleaning your house."

"Oh, yes."

"I'm sorry to call you at work . . ."

"Are you calling from the house?"

"No. I'm home."

"Home? Didn't you do the work?"

"Yes. Most of it. I did everything but the kitchen. And then I had to leave suddenly."

"Are you sick?"

"No."

"The baby."

She came close to accepting this as a way out.

"No."

"Then why?"

"It's something personal."

"I see."

"Can I pass by your shop to get paid? I worked five hours. That's $42.50."

"No. I'll see what you've done. I'll call you."

With that, she simply hung up.

Del knew that Mrs. Poole had heard the conversation, heard and listened. It was unavoidable on that floor unless you were making other noises, like watching TV. More tension. Mrs. Poole dispelled it later when she came back into the kitchen.

"Trouble?" she said.

"In a way."

"Anything I can do?"

"Not right now."

"Okay."

It was near six, just as they were about to serve supper, when Mrs. Roussel phoned.

"It was something personal all right, you have a lot of cheek, my husband caught you stealing."

"He did *not*!"

"He saw three movie tapes in your carriage. There's your pay."

"He didn't. If he did, why didn't he take them? I worked five hours, I want my money."

"He wanted to be sure. You don't deserve a nickel."

"And I don't want to go to your house to get it. Not with him there."

"What do you mean?"

"I didn't steal anything, he's lying."

"Why should he lie?"

"You wouldn't believe me."

"Why should I believe a thief?"

"You owe me for five hours' work."

"No! You helped yourself, plenty!"

Mrs. Roussel slammed down her receiver.

Del sat at the table, trembling, unable to say anything. Mrs. Poole came and stood by her and put an arm across her shoulders.

"Look, honey, it was going to be extra money anyway. You can do without it."

"It's not the money."

"I know. You want to come for a little walk? We can delay supper."

"No. And I'm not hungry. I mean, I can't eat."

"Well, I can. Do you mind if I do?"

"No, no."

Mrs. Poole got things ready, sat down, took a bite of the salad, and said casually: "Tell me."

It was still early in the day, after breakfast, and the other men, two new ones in the last four days, had their TV sets on. Martin Lacey was on his feet and busy, packing, not much of a job, but it was putting an end to the hospital routine. He was dressed in what he'd arrived in over two weeks ago, good work clothes, unsoiled, the kind of thing they sometimes advertise as leisure wear. A winter jacket and cap were on the bed, and next to them an elaborate tote bag with straps and Velcro, quite fashionable he surmised since it had been a birthday gift from his daughter. Into it went toiletries, a dressing gown, slippers, pajamas, odds and ends, all brought by Phil or Marge on their visits, familiar things, hardly noticeable at home but very evident here. He was relieved to stuff them into the bag. When he was ready, he sat down and gazed at the talk show on his neighbor's overhead screen.

In a while the head nurse, a Mrs. Boutiller, arrived with an orderly, a pleasant Southeast Asian, who was pushing a wheelchair.

"I don't need that," he said, thinking the orderly would simply go away.

"It's the way all our heart patients leave," said the nurse. "You'd be surprised how much energy it takes to get out of here."

"It's a lot simpler to walk."

"You're not going to give me a hard time, are you?"

"No." He laughed. "I'm not."

He put on his jacket, carefully got into the wheelchair, which he thought would move; it didn't, and the orderly put the tote bag on his lap. The nurse followed them to the elevator.

"Thanks for everything," he said to her.

"Good luck. And take it easy."

He admitted to himself that it was better with the chair. The elevator was crowded and reshuffled at every stop, the ground floor was busy, and they had a good distance to go to the main entrance. It was work, even sitting down, for he couldn't remain passive. He got out of the chair slowly, took his bag from the orderly and thanked him, and went through the automatic doors. The bag had grown a little heavier.

Outside, glad to be on his own at last, he noticed first the sunlight, then the progress spring had made, and finally his pickup, motor running, and Phil Baines waiting, straight-faced, next to the open passenger door.

"How you doing?"

"Fine. Sure looks nice out here."

It crossed his mind to do the driving, but that was unnecessary and it would only make the ride tense. Time later to find out what he could do. He put the bag at his feet and Phil took the wheel.

They went through heavy traffic, west and out of the city, and got on the freeway going north. The truck sounded noisier than usual and felt bouncier and seemed to be going too fast. The freeway and the speed it took dominated everything. He saw the back end of farms and bush that had been cut through and service roads and a few small businesses, but there was no time to look. To arrive at anything was to leave it.

In a half hour they were off the freeway, going slower, and on to a secondary road into countryside he knew.

"Did they," Phil said, now that they didn't have to shout, "did they tell you things you couldn't do?"

"It was pretty general. Take things easy, don't get overtired, don't worry, keep away from stressful situations, no excitement, things like that."

Phil just laughed.

"That's exactly it," Martin said. "Instant happiness, and you won't get a heart attack."

"Can't be done. Something else'll get you. The way they talk, you'd think you had to live forever."

And that was that for a while, Phil wasn't a talker.

They drove through Middleton and later East Windsor and a few miles beyond that they left the pavement for a dirt road that had improved in two weeks. Here it was different, and welcome, as good as walking, and he felt something close to elation. He knew all of it, where the side roads went, and how far places were, and who was there. He looked at everything.

"You can stay at our place for a while."

"Thanks, Phil, but I'd like to go home."

"Yeah. That's what we figured."

They turned at a crossroads and were soon passing Phil's farm and in about two miles he saw his mailbox this side of a culvert that was the turn-in to his place. Normally it would merely have caught his eye, unless he had mail or it was broken, but at that moment it existed noticeably.

The driveway was about six hundred feet long, lined on either side with big maples, and it needed gravel and scraping to level out the spring ruts. It led to an old two-story clapboard house, with a railed veranda in front and along the driveway side, set some two feet above the ground on a stone foundation that made for a leaky cellar. Attached to the house was a long shed, big enough to hold the winter's firewood and to serve as a garage. Past this were two more sheds and an unpainted barn with two big doors on rails.

They pulled up to where Phil's car stood in the driveway. Marge was on the veranda just outside the kitchen door, smiling, simply smiling, without effort or even knowing it.

"Well," she said in her somewhat high voice, "you're here."

"Yeah, still here."

"Aren't we all."

Marge was in her sixties. She was short and rounded, looking almost big in jeans and windbreaker, a getup that made her small features seem chubby, that and the glasses and the mass of brown graying hair she kept variously styled because hair had to look nice. She had an air of nervous energy about her and a look of impatience in her skeptical pale brown eyes.

They went into the kitchen, and Phil diplomatically carried in the tote bag and placed it in another room. Marge had a fire going in the big cookstove and two pots and a kettle on its large surface. She'd put order in the place and cleaned the floor.

"It looks different," said Martin, "a whole lot cleaner than when I left."

"Oh," Marge said, dismissing the compliment but enjoying her coup. "I had to throw a lot of stuff out of your fridge, but I brought over a few things."

"You shouldn't have bothered, I was looking forward to cleaning up."

She didn't believe him, she just laughed.

"I left things out so you wouldn't have to hunt for them."

On the electric stove was a clean fry pan and a double boiler, and on the work space next to it an egg lifter, a toaster now looking like new, plates, a mug. They were all familiar things, as was everything else, but they seemed distant. He'd been away longer than he realized.

"You lost weight," said Marge.

"Some, I guess. My clothes are a little loose."

"You can't afford that."

"Oh, I'll get it back."

They didn't refer again to his condition. Marge made instant coffee, and they sat at the table talking of things that had occurred while he was gone. The country habit was not to hurry a visit, except when it was obviously necessary, or to prolong it so that it began to interfere with the work that was always there to be done. It was an unspoken etiquette, crude and nosy to one who, like himself years ago, didn't know its depth, but it was subtle in its own way, it used no phrases or ceremony, it was action: you visited, you looked around, you chatted, you added it up and, if need be, you did something.

"Well," said Phil at one point, "we'd better be getting along."

It was the usual signal and it would take another while before it was actually done.

"I put two pies in your freezer," Marge said. "They're cooked, all you have to do is heat them."

"That's one of the first things I'm going to do."

She laughed. He noticed the firewood Phil had brought in. He knew they'd done a lot around the place, some of which he'd never discover.

When they were ready to leave, he saw them to their car.

"Thanks for everything," he said without going into it any further.

Phil merely grinned.

"We'll come by," Marge said.

He watched the car back up to the front of the house and swing down the driveway and on to the road. He stood for a time looking at the familiar landscape, hills on the horizon, places where forest had been cut, buildings a mile away to the west, plowed fields on his neighbor's farm, his own which he rented out, the quarter-acre garden that was ready for tilling, the lawns around the house just beginning to turn green, the big maples in bud, the driveway that needed scraping. He began to see all the work that had to be done. Home. And yet not home.

He went inside. There was lots to find out.

He unpacked and put away his things and placed his soiled clothes near the washer, trifling work, but he had to stop when it was done. It left him tired and anxious, the kind of feeling that makes you listen mentally for wrong notes and look over your shoulder for trouble. He wasn't too surprised, but he was disappointed. Being able to work was crucial.

"The first day's a big day, let it ride."

He said it aloud. For the first time in over two weeks he was alone, and at home. He had looked forward to it, had longed for it. But it had been abrupt, a car ride away from the busy activity of the hospital, goodbye, good luck, speed again, even in an old pickup, as if he were going, hurrying, back to normal. No, not to normal. He wasn't just solitary, or merely private, as he had been for the last five years, *that* he'd rather welcome. This time he was weak and restricted.

It was a complete turnabout. At the hospital there had been nothing he could do except cooperate when and how they wanted him to. They had made him virtually dependent. Here it was the opposite. Everything had to start and finish with him. There were no systems here, no fixed organization, nothing automatic, just the routines of work, which were, after all, simply him doing things. Without him they didn't exist, not food, or cleaning up, or making firewood, or repairing things, or making things grow. Without him active and busy, none of it was there or there for long.

"Let it ride."

It would mean being idle or killing time, both tedious. There was little to do inside. He had kept the house more or less the way it was when his wife was living, not as a memorial, that was too vague compared to the reality of existing, but because he admired her work and had enjoyed their teamwork and because it was too much fuss to change it. It was clean, which was important to him, and cluttered largely with tools and small repair jobs and books and scratch pads with memos and scribbled designs and clean dishes not put away because they were used three times a day. It looked disorganized, but he knew where everything was, and the scattered tasks gave him something to do when the weather was bad. But it wasn't bad now. And it was spring. He put on his jacket and went outside, wondering what he could safely do.

His place was quiet. The dirt road that passed some six hundred feet away was a back road giving access to the farms in the area. Most traffic on it was going to somebody's house or had some local purpose, the mailman once a day, the milk tanker, oil delivery once a month in season, the road grader from time to time after a rain, now and then a tractor pulling something, and regularly the cars and trucks of his neighbors. Even apart from that, it was rarely completely silent. There were always sounds, the wind especially, in many variations, and birds and frogs at night this time of year and the noisier insects and sometimes animals. The sounds had a meaning, a source, and you could identify them. When it was really silent, it was noticeable. You listened. It was like listening to existence.

At the storage shed at the back of the house he unlocked and slid the door open slowly on its track. On the side away from the house was a long workbench running under two windows. On it was a large vise, a drill, a grinder; farther down a radial saw, a variety of tools, two chain saws, one with a sharpening device clamped on it. On the floor was a tractor, some fifteen years old; next to it a gas lawn mower, then an eight-horsepower snowblower, and near the entrance a red rear-end tiller gleaming with the care that had been lavished on it all winter. On the walls hung more tools, belts, spare parts, extension cords, work lights, wire and useful junk, all in the open where he could keep track of it. It was neat and organized and practical, it had an atmosphere of work, the careful experienced work of a man with a lot of time on his hands.

The tiller had become a sort of symbol. It prepared the soil and kept the weeds down and cleaned up after harvest. It did the back-bending work of a lot of people, and he had no people, here. Without it nature would defeat him, with it he was a community of one. An ambivalent symbol. Still, he admired its ingenuity and function and power.

It started on the second pull and when he put it in low it idled smoothly. It accelerated without coughing or smoking, responded well to being in gear, and went very slow without missing. It was ready. But the two pulls had done it for him. It was all he could manage. He watched it run for a few minutes and turned it off. He was the one who wasn't ready.

He left the shed and began to stroll down the driveway, vaguely giving himself the purpose of checking the mail, which, he knew, wasn't there. Six hundred feet to the road was, not surprisingly, a long walk. The soft gravel wasn't a hospital corridor and work boots weren't slippers. It would be a criterion. When he could walk it as before, without thinking or noticing, he'd be back in trim. What was good now was simply being out in the open, and yes, alone, if you compared it to being in a room with three others, and seeing the sky in all directions and the things under it, right there and real, not shrunken and faked like the stuff on TV. Good just to be away from that, a twenty-inch fantasy with tinny speakers making more noise than a lifetime of emergencies. But you can't just be. You have to be doing something. There was no mail.

He got back to the house slowly. He realized where he stood. There wouldn't be anything doing for a while. He was all but powerless. The enforced idleness would lead to thinking, and that to worry, and from there to feelings that could lead nowhere but down. The facts were against him. No room at all for a facile optimism. Too much was missing.

When he checked the stove, he saw that Marge had left a stew simmering. It'd be good for at least three meals. Bless her.

Martin dialed the eleven numbers slowly, glancing from the phone to a card on the wall, waited as it rang, gave the operator his home number when she came on, and waited again. His daughter answered, and when they had talked awhile he gave her his news. He knew she'd be concerned and that her concern would come out as irritation.

"You should have phoned me."

"That would only have put you in suspense for nothing. Or made you come all the way from Toronto. I was really all right. If things had looked bad, Phil would've called you."

She was busy, he knew, and would have willingly postponed a crowded agenda. She was a financial analyst with an investment firm, had two girls, eight and ten, whom he saw once a year, rather awkwardly, by going there.

"Did they tell you what it was, what it is?"

"No. They don't quite know what it is. They only told me what to do." It was funny when you came right down to it.

"They must have said something."

"They said it was a heart attack."

"Oh."

"To take it easy, take naps, eat few fats, that sort of thing, and I'm doing it."

"How do you feel?"

"I'm getting stronger, slowly."

"I mean, what do you feel, any pain in the chest, short-winded . . . ?"

"No. Weak, but no pain."

"That's good. How are you making out?"

"Fine."

"I mean, are you able to cope, to look after things?"

"Sure, enough to get by."

He could sense her exasperation, getting by wasn't enough. Living like a hermit in the country could be tolerated, but reducing that to the level of getting by was pure obstinacy. It didn't matter how he phrased it, he knew how it would be heard. It was comical without being funny.

"Look, Dad," she said, "let me know, will you, if . . . when . . . if things get to be too much. I mean . . ."

"I know what you mean. I'll call you. I'm as cowardly as the next guy."

"I wish you were."

"Will you tell the others? I don't feel up to a lot of talking."

He had a second daughter in Edmonton and a son he rarely heard from.

"I'll tell Sue. And Ted, if I can find him."

"Yeah. I'll be in touch."

"Okay. Bye."

Stan timed it to arrive at the Ashton Elementary School just after the teachers got there and well before the school buses at 8:30. On two different days when he was sure the school's activities were well begun he had seen eleven cars parked in a neat row on the long side of the building. He had driven by at scattered intervals. It wouldn't have done to sit in the car and watch people arriving in the morning and leaving in the afternoon. A woman could do it, but he couldn't even dream of recruiting that kind of help. With luck he might catch the teachers together in one try. The cars were there, presumably the same ones, he hadn't checked the makes or licenses, and they probably represented the whole staff. He parked across the street, quite openly, went over to the school and into the big front entrance.

There was an office on one side of a wide vestibule and some sort of sitting room on the other. They seemed empty, it was a little early for normal business, but he walked right by without looking inside. That put him in a corridor that made a T with the vestibule. To his right he heard voices and a radio, went in that direction, came to an open door, by the look of it a teachers' room, and went in casually. There were more than eleven people, maybe fifteen, perhaps a third were men, no, seven were men. He ignored them and looked at the women, four were middle-aged, two had the wrong color hair, and the next two were people he'd never seen. Finally, over the chatter, one of the men said, "Hello, can I help you?"

"This can't be the principal's office."

"That's next door. You have a child here?"

"Oh, no. I want to see him about filling in."

"It's a she. I should tell you, though, there's a long list of substitute teachers."

"I guess that's the way it goes. Is this the entire staff?"

"The regular full-time staff." Like many a teacher, he liked to explain. "There's an art teacher who's part-time."

"Would she need any help?"

"It's a he. Help isn't what he needs, it's more work, by that I mean a broader program."

"Well, thanks anyway."

"Good luck."

"By the way, would you happen to know if an Adele Symons ever worked here?"

"Adele, Adele. I don't think so. How long ago?"

"The last few years."

"N-n-n, no. I'd remember. I've been here five years."

"Okay, thanks."

He found the principal's office and tapped on the open door. A stout woman in her forties was at a desk facing the entrance. She had a chubby pretty face, short light-brown hair set stylishly, and bright blue eyes which, when she pulled away the reading glasses, made her look naïve.

"Yes?"

"May I come in? I won't take up much of your time."

"I haven't got much of it to take up, the children'll be here any minute. Sit down."

He liked her. She had an air of reluctant toughness, as if she'd realized that a lot depended on how she stood up to things. He decided not to pose as anything.

"Could you tell me if a woman, Adele Symons, ever worked here? She'd be in her mid-twenties."

He imagined for an instant that her eyes became less naïve. Was it suspicion of him, or did the name evoke something?

"Could you describe her a little more?"

"Average height, she's slim, some'd say thin, almost reddish hair, auburn, longish face, straight narrow nose, and very light blue eyes."

He heard himself speaking slowly and sounding like a man remembering something sadly. He tried to keep it businesslike but his words carried memories.

"Does she have a teaching degree?"

"No. A bachelor's, in literature."

"And you?"

"Same thing. I knew her in college. And a little after." It sounded so innocent.

"That wasn't too long ago."

"A few years."

"She didn't work here."

"Oh." He pressed on. "She might have applied." He let it go as a suggestion.

"It's possible, a lot of people do. What's your interest in this girl?"

"She's a friend. I heard she was in these parts. I thought I'd look her up."

This time the eyes weren't naïve at all.

"There has to be more to it than that."

"There is. It's, well, personal."

"That's not too informative. In what way is it personal?"

"I know she's been through a rough time and I'd like to know how she's making out."

"That's all?"

"That's all right now. Until I find her, all I can do is wish."

"When did you see her last?"

"About two years ago."

"And you care?"

"Yes."

"Two years is a long time for just caring."

"I've had a little trouble myself."

"I'm sorry to be so prying, Mr. . . ."

"Hagan, Stan Hagan."

". . . Mr. Hagan, but this is a little unusual and I'm not sure I can be of help. Have you only started looking for her now?"

"No, three, four months ago."

"Here in Ashton?"

"Middleton, East Windsor, I got here about two weeks ago."

"Does anyone know you in Ashton?"

"Not really. My landlady. I had a talk with the police chief when I got here, to let him know I'd be . . . looking."

They were interrupted by the sound of motors and screechy brakes and the panic-level cries of children being themselves. She stood up, she was short, and looked out the window behind her.

"I have to go. You can wait, if you wish."

"I'll wait."

"There's a sitting room off the lobby."

He went there and waited, standing, looking out the window at the children, who were still arriving. They were less noisy now that he could see them. More buses arrived, and unloaded, and left. They were crude and cumbersome, and looked as if they'd been pressed into this last service before being towed to the junkyard. He got away from the window, kids see everything and invent rumors, he would be a cop, no, that's big city, an inspector, a parent, a man with a complaint, some teacher's boyfriend. He noticed an ashtray and lit a cigarette automatically. The principal either knew something or didn't, and she would tell or wouldn't. That's the logical estimate. Or she was indulging in a little soap opera, and that would be fantasy, no logic could touch that.

Somebody blew a coach's whistle, the noises stopped suddenly, the silence held for a while, another whistle, then shufflings and murmurings that eventually came inside the building and into the classrooms. He went back to the window. Fifteen minutes later she appeared in the doorway.

"Mr. Hagan."

He followed her back to the office. She indicated the chair he had occupied, took her place behind the desk, and fingered a 5 × 8 index card. It wasn't soap opera.

"Adele Symons applied here"—she looked at the card—"a little under a year ago, last August, just before the school year. There was no follow-up, by her or by me."

"Do you have an address?"

"Yes. It's care of Peterson, RR2, Ashton. No phone."

"Only the mailman would know where that was."

"That's what I said and she explained that it was on the road to Elizabethville. I made a note of it."

"Do you remember anything about her?"

"I'm trying to. It was quite a while ago. And since there was little chance of her being hired I didn't take much of a curriculum vitae. I have 'part-time' scribbled here. If I recall, she said she could only work part-time. I also have 'distraught?' with a question mark. She was nervous, I thought even desperate, but perhaps that was only about looking for a job. I didn't go into it. That's all I have."

He stood up to go.

"Was anyone with her?"

"I don't know."

"Did she come by car?"

"I don't know that either."

"Thank you for your help."

"That's all right. I hope you . . . look her up."

He nodded and left.

He went north out of Ashton on Route 131 toward Elizabethville. The RR2 address meant it was a roadside mailbox. He slowed for each one as he came to it, stopping at times and looking across the road at names visible from the opposite direction. Where there were no names, he pulled in and inquired. They weren't Petersons. He got farther and farther away from Ashton and had gone, he was sure, beyond the limits of the postal zone. He got as far as Elizabethville, some fifteen miles from Ashton, turned around and started back, double-checking. No Peterson. He was sure she hadn't given a phony address, she'd been looking for a job, she'd want to be reached.

In Ashton he stopped at a booth and used the phone book. There were two Petersons, each with a number and a street in town. He called them, they didn't know anyone on a rural route. He went to the post office, got the name and address, also rural, of the man who handled the route, decided against doing it by phone, and drove south to a farm just outside the town. He wasn't home, but his wife explained that there were back roads to Elizabethville and gave detailed and confusing directions meaningful only to a native. He understood enough of them to know how to get started. He drove north again, got back on Route 131 to Elizabethville, and just out of Ashton took the first turnoff right, onto a gravel crossroad.

He stayed on it for about two miles, checking every

box, came to another crossroad, still dirt, and turned right again, followed a curving road and soon found himself heading back to Ashton. On pavement and in town where the mailboxes disappeared, he U-turned and started out again for Elizabethville. He drove very slowly. There was nothing to be gained by hurrying, and he wanted to remember what ground he'd covered. The sure way would have been to wait for the mailman at his farm, but that would have meant a lot of explaining and a whole family of curious people. No hurry. Easy would have to do it.

In a half hour he came to a fork that had a narrow sign pointed at one end reading THREE MILE POND. He stayed on the main road and came into flat country that had a scattering of flimsy-looking summer places, still closed, and mobile homes on foundations, some on concrete blocks, others on banked earth, some with small trees that had been planted in the leveled-off frontage. He speculated that these places had access to Three Mile Pond. And as he brought his attention back to the mailboxes, he was looking at one that he could easily have missed. He was going slow and the light must have been right. He stopped and got out.

Decal letters had been painted over with one coat of white paint, and with that as background the name Lennox had been done in red carefully but not professionally. The old decals came through faintly behind the new name: P-T-R-ON. It was a mobile home, an old four-door Chevy in the driveway, and someone taking a look from the window to the left of the door. He went right up to it and knocked.

A man in his sixties, wearing a light bush jacket and slippers, opened up and looked at him.

"Hello," he said, not enthusiastically, "you looking for somebody?"

Behind him, a woman his age, presumably his wife, went from one side to the other to get a better look.

"I'm not sure if I've got the right person."

"Well, it's Lennox, like it says."

"That's just it. I was told that . . ." He didn't want to criticize the man's paint job. ". . . a man called Peterson lived out here."

"Oh, he used to," the woman said. She seemed to be standing on tiptoe. "Come on in where we can talk."

Mr. Lennox clearly didn't like the idea, but he stepped aside and let Stan go in. She led them through a narrow passage into a living room that managed to look normal because the furniture was small. The place was so clean it looked new.

"You sit over here," she said. "Would you like a beer?"

"No, thanks."

"Coffee, then?"

"All right, if it's no trouble."

"No, it's ready."

"I'll have a beer," Lennox said. And it was her turn not to like the idea. She went back through the narrow corridor.

"Do you know where Peterson is now?"

"He's in Florida," she called out from the next room.

"Couldn't wait to get away," said Lennox, "couldn't stand the winters. Had arthritis pretty bad, found it hard to shovel snow, and the cold got to him."

"He didn't stay around to sell the place," she said, still from the other room, "he had an agent do it."

She came in with the coffee and a glass of beer. Lennox drank it in two gulps and got up to get the rest of the bottle. As he poured, he seemed to lose his tension.

"Do you know how to get in touch with him?"

"No. We never saw him," she said. "Maybe the real estate person does."

"He's retired, like me. Retirement is for the goddam birds. So he probably keeps moving around. I know how he feels. Retirement is something they try to sell you, leisure, freedom, no responsibilities, no worries, all that crap. You know what retirement is? It's nothing. Just nothing. It's sitting next to your grave waiting to fall in. But you didn't come here to listen to my opinions, did you? You wanna know about Peterson."

"When did you buy the place?"

"About seven months ago," she said, "last October."

"That's eight months," said Lennox, "I've been counting."

"Was there someone else living here? A young woman?"

"Yes. There was a girl here when we came up to look at the place. We were with the agent. We didn't see much of her. The next time, she wasn't around. She left the place nice and clean. She didn't seem to have much."

"What makes you think that?"

"You can sort of tell. We looked at the place pretty closely and she didn't have much. I guess it took everything to look after the child."

Stan tried not show his surprise. He knew nothing of a child.

"She had a child with her?"

"Well, I never saw the child," she said, "but there were baby things everywhere, a crib, and diapers, and stuff in the fridge."

"You don't know how old the baby was?"

"No, but judging by the nighties and things, I'd say somewhere around six months old."

He began immediately to think back, but he couldn't get by the confused and painful memories. He caught himself and kept talking. Still, he knew without any confusion that she had left about two years ago, she had to.

"Did she have a car?"

"I don't know."

"No car," said Lennox. "The place looked deserted when we drove up."

"Would anyone around here know her?"

"You're looking for her," he said, "not Peterson, uh?"

"Yeah. But I wish I could talk to him too, he'd know something about her. He seems to have given her a break."

"He gave us a break, on the price," she said.

"How about the neighbors? Could any of them have known her?"

"Kay Saunders," she said, "just next door." She gestured to her right.

He thanked them and left and walked the few hundred feet to the next mobile home. It was older and had been there longer. It had a lawn, still light green and thick with new growth, bushes beginning to leaf, two trees about eight inches across, and a flower bed running the length of the place except at the step-up porch in the middle. The driveway was flat stones like a patio, just long enough to hold a car, after which it became a path to the porch. On it was a mud-streaked red Honda waiting for the rain to clean it.

As he got there, a wiry old woman in jeans and a windbreaker came out of the house and met him on the lawn. She must have been close to eighty.

"I lost track of her," she said. Her voice was thin and clear, and her tone was disappointed. Mrs. Lennox must have phoned ahead.

He wondered if the old lady were dismissing him or just stating a fact.

"I'm sorry to hear that, Mrs. Saunders. When did you see her last?"

She looked at him steadily, dark brown eyes in a wizened face partly hidden by flowing white hair, no glasses. She seemed genuinely sad about something.

"When I drove her into town to her new place."

"Do you remember the place?"

"Of course I do. But it won't do you any good, she's not there. I took it for granted we'd be staying in touch, but we didn't. The one time I told myself to mind my own business and now I don't know where she is. By the time I made up my mind to visit her, that was a month later, she was gone."

"Where was the place?"

"It won't . . ." she began to repeat herself and stopped. "It's 265 Cartier Street. It's empty. The woman who lived there got too feeble to run it, so they put her in a home, and her relatives want to sell the place, but she doesn't want to, it's her last hold on something. Adele found another place, I guess, or left town. I wish I knew."

"Did she have a job?"

"Odd jobs, part-time, she didn't want to leave her baby."

He wanted to ask about the child, but a blunt question would have been too obvious.

"How long was she next door?"

"About four months. Peterson didn't want to leave the place empty, so he let her live there."

"Do you know how she met him?"

"No. She didn't say. She didn't say anything about herself. Young people don't tell you things, maybe they're afraid you'll pump them dry. She paid her way, in kind. She took nothing for nothing. If I lent her the car she did my shopping for me; if I baby-sat the little one, she'd clean up my house for me. She didn't have a penny to spare, but she'd put gas in the car if there was no other way of paying me back. Independent, proud maybe, but not snotty, she was determined to make it on her own for some reason. I think of her a lot, I miss her. She wasn't running away from you, was she?"

Not anymore, not here, were the words that jumped to mind, but he said: "No. By now I probably don't exist."

"Don't be too sure."

"Oh?"

"Just a general feeling. She exists for you, doesn't she?"

"Yeah."

"You'll let me know if . . ."

"Yeah."

"I really mean it. I want to know."

"So do I."

Then, without thinking, he decided to be blunt.

"What did she call the baby?"

"Elizabeth. Betty. And all kinds of pet names."

"How old was the baby then?"

"Six months, when they moved. She'd be just over a year now."

He could see that Kay Saunders was thinking. So was he.

"Thanks for talking to me."

He walked back to his wagon and, not to have to pretend he didn't see them, he waved a hand at the Lennoxes, who were watching from their living-room window. He drove back to town and found the address on Cartier Street.

There was nothing there except a for-sale sign on one of the porch posts. The relatives must have prevailed, or the feeble old lady had died. The neighbors on each side knew nothing of a young woman and a child who might have lived there for a short time six months ago.

3

❦

In little more than a week Del lost one customer, a Mrs. Davis. Del had felt that something was up, but it took the event to confirm it. That whole day, a Monday, the woman had been hovering around, something she never did, and when she was paying Del in late afternoon, she explained rather nervously that her sister was coming to live with her and that she, the sister, would look after the housecleaning. It was plausible and total, the work would be taken care of, there was nothing to discuss. Del didn't quite believe it, but she could hardly cross-examine Mrs. Davis.

That Wednesday she lost another one, Mrs. Melling. This time it was a niece who was going to do the work. And the woman, who talked a lot, couldn't help adding, "And don't use my name for a reference, I've stopped giving references."

Del took it up immediately. "Have you been giving very many?"

"No. That is, some. I mean, I don't know you all that well and I couldn't really say what kind of person you are."

"Did someone ask you?"

"No. No, no one asked, no one at all."

"Did someone call you?"

"I don't give references, that's all, I don't care who calls."

Del let the matter drop, it would only lead to a squabble.

She was down to six customers in her three-week cycle. Losing two was a serious drop in income. Losing them suddenly and one right after the other made her wonder if there was anything behind it. But all she could do was wonder, she had no way of really knowing.

She stopped wondering the following Friday.

It was a warm day, now late May, sunny at eight o'clock. She was wearing jeans and a light jacket and, as always, had Betty in the stroller. She was going north on Township Street, to turn at a street three blocks past City Gardens, and stopping from time to time to adjust the load in the stroller and to retrieve things that Betty dropped. Slowly a combination of minor circumstances made her alert: vaguely noticed cars accelerating after slowing up for something, drivers honking one after another to get by a slowpoke, the odd pedestrian hesitating for a car that might be moving but wasn't just yet. It was a pattern, repeated, and it finally clicked with her. She had straightened up after stooping over the stroller and happened to look back for the moment. She saw a pale blue car idling at the curb some fifty feet behind her. The passenger window seemed to be down. She couldn't see the driver past the reflections on the windshield. She didn't have to see him, she was fairly certain who it was.

When she moved, it moved. She walked half a block, stopped, pretended to be busy with the stroller, didn't look directly but saw that the car was still there. She did it twice more. The car was always with her. She wondered, apart from the obvious, why he'd be following her. And even before the question was fully formed, she knew: to find out who her customers were. The two she'd lost were known, she'd left their phone numbers with Mrs. Roussel. She'd also left her own, but without Mrs. Poole's name. Even then, it would be easy to call and find out. But Mrs. Poole wouldn't give information to strangers. He'd have to follow her to find out where she lived. How did he know she'd be on Township Street at eight in the morning? With that line of thought, she was beginning to find it hard to stay calm.

When she arrived at the street she wanted, she didn't take it but crossed it and stayed on Township. At the first house that had a walk and a hedge, she turned in without hesitation, went to the front of the stroller and busied herself with the baby. She had hardly begun when the blue car appeared.

She didn't look at it. She could see it was there, the passenger window down, fully stopped, the other traffic honking, a head bobbing inside to catch the address. She started unloading and getting ready to go into the house. The car began to move on. She risked taking a look and saw enough of him to be sure. She kept her head down, pretending to be busy, until she could no longer see the car. Then quickly she put things back, spun the stroller around, hurried to the corner, and ran to the house she wanted. She went her usual way, round the back where there were less stairs and where, if he came looking, he couldn't see her, and in by the kitchen.

It was disturbing. It hounded her all day. If he could find out where she worked, he'd have her fired. She surmised that he didn't know where she lived, that earlier he must have followed her home along Township but not into Station Street, which was a short street with houses only on one side and he'd be conspicuous. And if that were so, then he'd be trying again when she finished work.

At four she approached Township Street cautiously. She tried to account for every parked car, every slow car, no matter the color. None aroused her suspicions. From time to time she turned the stroller to face the curb as though she were going to cross Township and was able to get a good look at the traffic. It was light and moving. At Station Street she took the corner quickly and tried to walk normally, looking straight ahead. It was like expecting spiders to fall on you in the dark. She ran up the driveway, tucked the stroller out of sight, and peered around the side of the house. No blue car, no cars at all, trucks at the freight depot minding their own business.

She did her chores and made tea, put the baby next to her in a playpen, and sat, almost shaking, trying to make sense of what was happening. Around 5:15 she started to get supper ready, and some time after 5:30 Mrs. Poole came home and Del told her about the car.

"You're sure it was him?"

"Oh, yes! I sneaked a look when he drove off. It was him all right."

"And he didn't come back."

"Not then, I don't think."

"I mean after work."

"I didn't see the car, that car. They have two of them. He could have done it on foot, parked the car somewhere, anything. But he didn't know where I was exactly. And he wouldn't want to stand around too long. So he . . ."

"All right, all right. Don't let it build up. He probably didn't come back."

"He will. It's creepy."

In the evening as they were working on the knits they'd be showing at the Fashion Fair, the phone rang over the noise of the knitting machines and Mrs. Poole answered it and handed it to Del.

Evalynn Roussel identified herself.

"It's been difficult getting help. My husband says he's willing to give you another chance. I'm sure we can work something out. What do you say?"

All Del could manage was an incredulous whisper, "No."

Slowly she hung up the phone. She quoted the words verbatim, three times, to Mrs. Poole. She still couldn't believe it.

Mrs. Poole said, "He tricks his wife into turning up the heat. Very smart."

* * *

They pulled up at the Davis house, Del's Monday customer, and Mrs. Poole rang at the front door.

Mrs. Davis, a stout, cheerful woman, said, "Yes?" pleasantly to Mrs. Poole and, "Oh, hello, Del."

"May we come in?" said Mrs. Poole.

"Yes, I suppose so, but what . . . ?"

"Just for a little talk."

As Mrs. Davis was about to lead them into the living room, Mrs. Poole said, "Oh, let's sit in the kitchen, country-style, it's easier to talk that way."

"Can I get you some coffee?"

They said no, and Mrs. Poole explained that Del lived at her place, had been with her for some seven months, and that she knew her well enough to do what she was now doing.

"It's about last Monday," said Mrs. Davis sadly.

"Yes."

"Well, I . . ."

"It's nothing against you," Mrs. Poole hastened to say. "I'd just like to ask a couple of questions. You see, we know a few things you might not've heard about."

"All right. Ask them."

"Did a Mrs. Roussel phone you and say that Del had stolen things?"

Mrs. Davis thought it over worriedly and looked at Mrs. Poole and at Del. "Yes, she did."

"And that's why you let Del go?"

"Yes." She added quickly, "I had no reason not to believe her."

"Of course not. Did you know that she phoned another of Del's customers?"

"No."

"Did you know that the two girls before Del, Del makes three, to work at Roussel's were supposed to have stolen things?"

"No."

"From the husband?"

"No."

"Well, it's his story. Nobody stole anything."

"Then why is she doing it? She sounded sincere."

"She is. Let's put it this way: the man's got his wife fooled."

"Oh." Mrs. Davis thought it over. "I still have to believe her. I mean, she has some standing in this town. And I also believe you, don't get me wrong, and you too, Del. But I'd like to have more to go by than your just denying it, if you see what I mean."

"Of course."

Del didn't say a word, not even about getting her work back. Mrs. Poole talked up the fair and they left.

"That blackball carries a lot of weight."

Del agreed.

At Mrs. Melling's, the Wednesday customer, they presented the same case and got the same reaction.

After that, they drove to an EvaLynn store and Del waited in the car as Mrs. Poole went in. She came right out. They tried a second store, same thing. At the third she didn't come out for quite a while.

When she did, she explained: "I fibbed. I said that too many people had been pilfered, some broken into, inside jobs, and that we'd gotten together to see if we could connect anybody to any of those houses. And on and on. So she gave me the names of the two girls, the ones before you, with phone numbers. First names, Pauline and Beatrice."

"They won't want to talk about it," Del said.

"They would to you, you know what they've been through."

"They might."

"I told her about the fair, she said she always goes."

Martin was up around 5:30, dawn in late May, responding, it would seem, for he felt nothing special, to the appearance of the sun. Old men get up early, that's all there is to it, no point making a cosmic theory about it. Yet the day, another day, was there, solid with light, moving on, not to be called back, and this he felt so clearly it almost had him hurrying. He washed and shaved and straightened out the bed and had breakfast and rinsed the dirty dishes in hot water. It looked like routine, old habits grown automatic. But it wasn't. His first impulse was not to wash, not to shave, not to clean up, and that would have been the habit, and a hard one to break, a mess, and a drop in spirits. So the routine was deliberate, chosen, decided upon daily, with breaks now and then. At times the negative impulse made him feel like a teenager who hated to get up in the morning. Rebellion, second adolescence. It was supposed to make you feel young. That always drew a chuckle. Young is not noticing. He noticed.

It was over an hour before he could get outside. That was twice the time he normally took. He noticed that, too. The light was strong and still low, just past seven, and warm. It contoured the whole countryside and made every sort of pale green stand out against the shadow of every tree and bush and hollow. It showed up fence posts and the roads and rocks and cattle recently put out and buildings miles away. The backlit maples were black on one side and glowing on the other, and the driveway under them shone between the shadows of their trunks. Everything looked closer and realer, very much there, ready for something. And the birds, chattering and fussing and always on the move, made it all look busy and like a lot of fun. A dry cloudless warm morning. The way the sheds looked in that light and the way his shadow fell as he slid open the big door made it unmistakably late spring. A feeling of warmth to come, promise, a fruition in the offing, the sharp clear taste of work that would yield something. Hard work.

Very deliberately, with the least muscular effort and no hurry at all, he got the tiller running with two pulls of the starter cord. He waited a little, both to let the engine warm up and to get used to the idea of being so deliberate, and set it in motion. It had powered wheels that could move at two speeds, the faster that of a slow walk. Without that, he couldn't have used it, it weighed some three hundred pounds. He guided it down the driveway a little, then across the lawn and into the fenced-off garden. And there again he waited.

The garden looked forbidding, and inviting. It was big, a hundred by a hundred feet, a quarter acre, a lot for one man to tend. Weeds had sprouted all over. It was already late in the season. Usually by now it was all laid out and planted. But this time all he'd managed, exploiting last fall's preparation, was a few rows of peas and carrots, early things that could stand cool weather, and he'd done that gingerly, slowly, down on one knee like a man trying to pick cigarette ash off a rug. But the rest of it was green with weeds, it needed tilling. Nature never waited, it gave you no time, in its own way nature was time.

He started in. He set the tines for maximum depth, gassed the engine a little more, and engaged the forward lever. The machine did the work, he could guide it with one hand on a straightaway. It left behind it a wide strip of churned, leveled-off dark earth six to eight inches deep that would have taken hours of forking and raking to achieve. It always delighted him. What had been a chunky mass, caked and heaved by months of cold and snow, full of unwanted growth, became delicate rich soil ready for working. He could smell it and feel it and admire its appearance in the morning light. It was good to be doing it, and he had chosen to try.

The heavier work came at the end of the row. There, in order to turn, he slowed the engine, lifted the machine by the long handlebars until it was balanced on its two wheels, still rolling, and swung it right around to head back on a strip of untilled earth. It was a clean simple operation, and he had done it so often he could do it without thinking. And that was the trouble. He had to lift it and heave it and let it down. And he did it non-stop out of habit. It was too much. He realized he'd have to do the turning in phases, and not for long. He tried it at the end of the next row. It was awkward and out of rhythm, but it was easier. A job that could have been done in a few hours would now take days. He was on a different time.

From the shed he brought out a wooden box and put it in the garden's main path, which ran east-west, and used it to sit on. He felt silly doing that, the tiller idling in low, the earth waiting under the colorful sun, two passes made, one as row, the other as path, a trifle compared to the fifty-odd passes that would be needed. Silly, but necessary. He thought of doing alternate passes, tilling only the rows to be planted and leaving the paths untilled, but there the ground would harden and the weeds would take over and in the end it would mean more work. It was either do it all the way or don't do it at all. Even parcels that would lie fallow for the season had to be tilled, cover-cropped, tilled again, or in that one season it would grow so wild you'd never know there'd been a garden there. Nature's always at work, usually against you, unless you do something to make it go your way. And do it right. A hard fact. He never ceased to marvel at it, pointless and comic to complain, and, equally, rewarding to accept. And to work. He rested for ten minutes, tilled for another ten, four passes' worth, and sat down again, a little more tired than before.

It was hard to know how far he should go. Normally in the momentum of working he'd just keep going until the job was done. A day's work was a day's work, you took it for granted. But the momentum was now a risk. He knew he couldn't keep it up even for one morning. Not today. Tomorrow, a little more, if the weather held. Still more the next day. It was going to get done, somehow. And it wasn't a matter of decision or courage or grim effort under pain. Character had little to do with it, except to increase the risks. It was a matter of judging the safe side of physical limits. Hard to do, even if he'd been a doctor. But in the next half hour he had his answer. He was tired and sweaty and he could hear his heart thumping. To get tired at all meant being quickly exhausted. Judgment. And a clear decision, not easy. The work would have to wait. He steered the tiller back to the shed and left it there, uncleaned.

He didn't want to go inside, it didn't seem right. The time and the season and the kind of life he was living all meant being outdoors doing things. Being inside was for later, it came after something, it meant the work was done or the day was over or the season had come to an end. None of that had happened, it was still morning, still late May, and work, not done, was stopped. The best he could do was be there and be outside. And let things sink in. There was lots of handwriting on the wall.

He strolled very slowly along the driveway, under the maples, heading toward the main road and the mailbox, not going anywhere. Never on normal days would he do that, and rarely without some purpose, to get the mail or check the ruts or talk to someone in private if there were people in the house. When his wife was alive, they would walk there on summer evenings as the sun went down, not realizing how short the time was. And after that he simply avoided it. It was pointless alone. But when he was back from the hospital he had tried it over and over again, just to be able to do it, to get stronger, to be able to work. It all took time. The driveway stopped being a driveway then and became a lane covered with gravel, sand and stones packed down over the earth, changing with rain and wind, felt underfoot, wet and soft, dry and hard and dusty, and a car could pass on it all right, but that seemed secondary, a mere use that gave it a functional name while it remained very much itself, unnoticed, except by children and those who had been brought to it. Unusual to see it that way, and unwise to talk about it, you'd need a very special conversation for that, rare indeed, but he knew he was seeing it real. And in that moment, those moments, it all ceased being his. By legal concept it was, of course, no one could take it away from him, he could summon police and lawyers and judges to its defense, and he could bequeath it as he chose, that was all true, all valid and practical and not to be ignored, but despite all that, in those moments of insight, he could feel no ownership, and, more sharply, no familiarity. The lane and the trees and the land, the house, fences, all of it, like the sky, not his. It was as if he'd been newly placed there, granted some use, allowed some tenancy, temporarily, not home, not at all. It was more acute than seeing it for the first time, it was seeing it in its own context, not his, past the mental baggage of habit and culture and use. And seen that way, it simply left him. And he was there, emphasized, alone, moved to his very self, feeling something close to fear, yet, strangely, not upset. It felt like discovery. What held that held him.

And yet the fact was that he'd owned the place for over thirty years. He'd acquired it when the children were still children. Incredible that such time had gone by, it really did seem like yesterday. The truisms were true, that's how they got to be truisms. Mere time would bring that about, the experience of how fast and brief it all is, it was nothing special. What struck home was that the very place which had once represented so much human promise had come now to symbolize a real emptiness, a sort of human desert. He and his wife had simply plunged into the work of making a home for the children, seeing to their growth over the years, always with the vague expectation, never really expressed, that it would develop into something: a human harvest of some kind, a flowering and a handing on of some hard-won thing, a community so obvious it had to come about.

But it was not to be. Imperceptibly, time and cultural pressure dissolved it. Naïve to have a family at all, let alone three children, even more so to hope for a human continuity. The adult children left, of course, indeed had left in spirit since before high school, an empty city house was sold, he retired from his work, and he and his wife moved to the country. Nothing unusual in that, it was quite normal, it was even regarded as desirable. But the family had evaporated. It was down to visits, letters, a few phone calls, the pre-packaged rites of holidays and anniversaries. No complaints, no blame to lay, no one held responsible. It was time and nature and the way we live. But it was more than a letting go, it was also a falling off. Something that should be was not there. And that, for it was too subtle to give voice to, had to be accepted in silence. The beginnings of the desert.

It was all part of being human, of having lived. He was father, which had been a long task, and grandfather, which seemed to be a circumstance, and for some reason all of it was devoid of meaning. It was only a matter of biological fact, something for the children's medical records. It wasn't something he could actively be. It was as if it had never happened. Age wipes it all out. In practice he was a man living on a pension and puttering around in the country because he liked it that way. No more. All the experience, the work, the know-how, the loyalty, the hard-won knowledge, the human roles, the almost forced-upon-him wisdom, all that went for nothing. It just didn't exist—a blank and a gap so huge as to remove identity from him. He was culturally disreputable. Just another old guy who'd need help soon, a nuisance, a burden, they had organizations to process people like him, they would stereotype him to death. To hell with the culture. Another wilderness.

Bleak thoughts on a shining May morning. A morning without work. The lawns were getting overgrown, another problem. The lilacs were still in bloom, pungent, bushes as tall as apple trees, making a low roaring noise, like a good fire, with the buzzing of uncountable bees. Something was right.

He went back to the tiller for another try.

But it didn't work out. It was only a strong wish. He was loath to abandon the routines he'd built up. He was only going through old motions. And he realized it.

Stan was doing what he'd done in the other towns. At opening and closing times he checked the factories, the schools, the bigger stores, the banks, on a weekend the churches. He had them marked off on the town map, unnecessarily, but it passed the time and kept him to the task. The commercial streets he did at other times, mid-morning and mid-afternoon, working here and there in short segments so that he wouldn't be seen going from store to store and have people start noticing him. He looked at everything and everybody. It had become routine, except that most of what he saw was new.

He ate in inexpensive busy places, and now, a Wednesday, a week after he'd come to naught, he had lunch at a homemade fast-food stand limited to hot dogs and french fries and soft drinks, and looked over the staff and the customers inside and in their cars. After that, on foot, he went to every store and hang-out on the block and into the side streets, where, careful not to talk to them, he saw pre-school children, too old of course, but they caught his attention, and came across a few scattered kitchen-table operations in clothing and shoes and TV repairs and photo supplies, the kind of place that wouldn't hire anybody but might barter services.

By five o'clock he was outside a children's wear factory, made over from a large duplex, a branch of a larger outfit, probably piecework, and watched some two dozen women leave, not slowly, and saw no one he could recognize. He went back to one of the main streets where lots of people would be walking, stood on three different corners, checking every likely face, and saw nothing but complete strangers. Near six, when everybody else seemed to have gone home, he shook off the subtle promises of the two bars he kept seeing and got back to his imitation motel on Mill Street.

This was always a bad time of day. Work, or what looked like it, had to cease, and for the way he was living, leisure was mere delay, so much time to kill. He was tired, and hungry, worn down by the day's uneventfulness, and alone now to think about it. The atmosphere around one's self. He knew what he was into, a mood on the edge of self-pity, the urge to give it all up, the hundred reasons why, the desire to ease things, the compelling illusion of release that would come with a drink. One was enough to do it. It would trigger all the rest. He'd been there over and over again, into that heavy nothingness, and he wanted to stay on this side of it. He had learned not to fight his feelings, not to listen to their voices. They would lift, like fog, no matter how long it took. He'd had to learn other things as well, all humiliatingly obvious, like not letting himself get too hungry. Food or drink.

He dumped half a can of beans into a small double-boiler, set it cooking, made a crude undressed salad with cucumber and lettuce and a pale tomato, took the bread from the fridge, and laid out a place on the swing-up table near the back window. Banal, simple tasks which he wouldn't have done less than a year ago. They were still a willed set of actions, not habitual, a conscious routine in which there was safety and survival. Strange that living should be so difficult. He turned on the radio to have noises other than his own, took a long shower while the food got warm, and finally sat down to it, eating slowly, not unenjoyably, and watching the early-evening light change the landscape outside. He had coffee and a cigarette, cleaned up right after to avoid the depressing effect of dirty dishes, made another cup of coffee, and, back at the table, spread out the worn and heavily marked map of Ashton. Tomorrow's work.

The child haunted him. He could still feel, as though it were happening anew, the expectation aroused by Kay Saunders's information, and also the disappointment that followed. It was the first time he'd spoken to people who'd actually seen her, who'd known her. Much more real than a Christmas card, the child still more. But the card was more recent by six, even seven, months. What felt like a real advance was a step backwards. Three months, three towns. In a few days more he'd cover Ashton, but this time he'd have to stay and begin another, more concentrated search. He'd have to get a job to pay for it, and that would restrict his movements and delay things. Another month in another town. Easy now. It's not month by month, it's day by day. There might be another Kay Saunders.

When the radio fanfared the station's letters and proclaimed the time, 8 p.m., he turned it off, gathered his soiled clothing into a dark green plastic bag, grabbed a box of detergent, took it all to the wagon, and drove to a coin wash on Township Street. Three of the five washers were going and a fat woman sat mending something near the door, where it was cooler and less stuffy. It was a warm evening, the anticipated summer of late May which could still turn to frost overnight. He unloaded the bag into the machine, sprinkled in what he thought was enough detergent, figured out the dials once again, put in coins, and got the thing going. He did it almost angrily, it was a chore he had never learned to accept with indifference. The woman laughed, heartily and helplessly, at the comedy he was supplying without knowing it.

"I guess you don't do it very often."

"Once a week, usually," he said, glaring at the washer.

That set her off again. She must have thought bachelors were funny. He grinned at her amusement.

"The other way," he said, "is to buy enough clothes for a month, but that's too expensive."

More laughs.

"Men," she said.

He put the box of detergent in the wagon and stood outside looking at the night life on Township Street. The supermarket was still open, Wednesday night, he made a note of it, traffic was people driving instead of walking, a few teenagers clustered outside a restaurant, they were quiet and glum, farther down the street at the alleyway of the old hotel two bikers were displaying their machines to four or five envious onlookers, and farther still on the far side of the street a sign whose lights he couldn't read at this angle. He walked in that direction. The other stores were closed but lit inside, city hall was dark except for the police station on the side, the post office had lights shining on it from the lawn. The sign he'd seen was ROBIN'S and it advertised nude dancers. He went in.

The lobby, which was a vestibule a little wider than the doors, had photographs on two walls, girls who worked there and on the circuit. It took time to get used to the one dim bluish light. He examined them all. No one he knew, but the pictures weren't meant to show faces. He pushed his way inside and went to the bar. Tables and people and the same dim light, an unlit four-by-four stage, no dancers, disco music from somewhere, a few people moving to it on a bare spot on the floor, young topless waitresses with mechanical smiles that were wasted here but might move them up to a bigger town. He checked the people near the waitresses, it was a natural place to be looking.

"Yeah?"

The bartender was late thirties, hard-looking as though he'd practiced, in a stylish open shirt, medallions on a neck chain, with an air that said he was the boss saving a buck on a slow night. He glanced at Stan's plain shirt and windbreaker.

"Coke."

"You mean like Pepsi?"

It was a straight-faced joke. Neither of them laughed.

"That's it."

"Anything in it?"

"Nothing, I'm going slow."

"How slow?"

"Very slow. Booze isn't my thing."

"You don't say. Looking for somebody?"

"No. Waiting. It might not happen."

"That's the way it goes."

He served up a Coke in a small glass, took the two dollars from the bar, didn't make change, and disappeared or seemed to. It was a lot to pay for a Coke, the price of lunch in some places, but it was either that or get thrown out. She might be working at night. Anywhere. He didn't like the idea, but broke is broke and money is money. He sipped the drink, looked at his watch, and by following the girls managed to take in everybody. Nothing. Just the noise, the fun that had a touch of grimness, and the acrid smoke. The place depressed him. He stayed long enough to finish the drink without hurrying and walked out.

At the coin wash he waited for the machine to stop, moved the small load to the dryer, got that going, tried to sit and wait, but gave up and went outside again.

The supermarket was closing, the teenagers were still outside the restaurant, some sitting on the curb, the bikers were gone, the street looked darker with fewer people. He was alone on his side of the street, lit by the fluorescent glare of the laundry, and perhaps conspicuous, certainly noticeable, especially without the fat funny lady to make things look normal. He knew a lot about normality, the way a lazy man knows a lot about work, he had watched it for months. He moved away from the light, down the street to his right and across, and into the old hotel, where to the right of the main entrance a sign said BAR over a wide wooden door.

It was really a tavern. The bar was a counter from which waiters got beer for the customers. The place was vast, big enough to hold a barn dance, and all of it was made of wood, floor, walls, ceiling, off plumb and sagging, it might have been a ballroom a century ago, now filled with round enamel-topped tables on cast-iron bases, chipped and scratched, each surrounded by four or five small wooden armchairs. At the far end was most of the action, the baseball game on TV. The clientele was largely male, a few older women long since liberated. He sat at a vacant table and tried to make out some of the ball game.

A heavyset waiter came over unhurriedly. "What'll you have?"

"Nothing, thanks."

"Okay by me."

"Just looking around. I got laundry up the street."

"Any time."

This was normal. A casually indifferent waiter, no front, no special slang, no covered-up sales, no keeping an eye out for the law. Everything was human, a little sloppy, no tragedies in the offing, just the usual burdens of living. It was just about right. Except that a beer would go well with it. The desire wasn't physical, like wanting to eat, it was mental, like wanting to be happy. No crisis, yet he wasn't kidding himself or playing with anything, there was nothing sneaking up on him, but he had no reason to be here except to kill time, and the purpose of the place was drinking. Normal, but not for him. In a flash, without even thinking, he could say to hell with it and signal the waiter to come over. It had happened before and he'd learned to be afraid of it. Get up and go now, don't debate it, you'll lose.

He went back to the Laundromat and put money in the dryer, which had stopped, and sat down under the lights to wait in the damp heat for his clothes to dry. Normal. You're being ironical, he told himself, and that's close to self-pity.

The dryer was a commercial model with a big round heavy window that let you see the clothes tumbling inside. It rumbled and whirred, monotonous with electrical energy, loud in the low-ceilinged space. He watched the clothes flying around, it was the only activity in the place, and he felt taken in by somebody's bright idea, give them something to see and they'll use it by the hour, put in a Coke machine and it'll be a community center. All you wanted was dry clothes, not entertainment. Hicksville, that's what it is. Easy now. It may be Hicksville, but this stuff's from the big city, it's sophisticated design, you're being suckered by psychology, see the nice clean clothes tumbling. He laughed it away.

It wasn't the dryer that bothered him, it was the whole day, the streets, watching other people's lives, the make-believe motel, the club, the tavern, here. This and two other towns just like it. Hicksville, I tell you. So? Where do you want it to be? I don't want it to be anywhere. You can't have it that way, it's got to be somewhere. The place is always here and the time is always now. In Hicksville? You better get off that track, there's no such place as Hicksville, not today, today everybody knows about everything, a small town is a piece of big city. Yeah. A tavern in a decrepit hotel full of small-time boozers. And I walk out. You're damn right, you walked out. What did you want? Show them what big-time drinking is? Other people can drink, let them drink, you don't have to resent it. The macho's gone, there's no macho on your knees, much less on your face. Yeah. True. A hard boy in a junk shop playing big man. A Coke's like asking for a glass of milk. So ask for it, you're not in that league anymore. She wasn't there. That's a break. With hard boy and his latest clothes she'd never get loose. I don't know that she *is* loose. I'll bet he never comes in here, he probably buys new clothes every second day. Why not every day, you poor damn fool, what the hell is he to you? Nothing. Nothing at all. He was there, that's all, now he's here, send him away.

That left himself. And the dryer, and the peculiar sense that goes with being alone. Not just private, alone. Private is with other people, they there, you here. Alone is just you, here. It has a touch of chaos to it. When you're busy at something, you don't notice it much. But when you're doing nothing, or worse, when you've been brought to that, then you're just you, just existing, inside. And that has a strange way of not feeling right. You could just as easily not be. It feels that fragile. You go to great lengths to avoid it, not to come to know, plan ahead to keep busy not to meet yourself. But you're really there all the time, just you, waiting. It's just a matter of when.

The first time was a shock.

They were standing at the foot of the bed, two men in their thirties, one tall and large, the other tall and slim, both pleasant and calm. The bed was a hospital bed. The light was dim and too bright, the walls sky-blue.

"What are you guys doing here?"

"You called us," the large one said.

"I called you?"

"That's right. That was a couple of days ago. We found you in a Laundromat. You were naked. You put all your clothes in the washer and you were trying to climb in and two cops were keeping you from doing it and trying to keep themselves from laughing at the same time. And trying to keep from getting dirty. You were pretty messy. They each had you by a hand, like a dance of some kind, crazy. Then you faded away, and had the twitches. So, instead of the slammer, they got us an ambulance. They were good about it. That makes you lucky. Here they gave you things to cut the shakes and the runs and the rest of it, they're feeding you vitamins, no drugs, your arms said no."

"I called you."

"Yeah. How else? We found your place, door open, phone book open, but no you, just a mess. So we figured you weren't far. We followed the mess. You called all right."

"I don't remember."

"That fits."

"Nothing about the washer either."

"Yeah."

"Trying to clean myself. That's symbolic."

"Could be. But don't give us too much of that, that's poor me as hero."

"What the hell do you know about it?"

"Three years ago I was where you are, giving two other guys the same bullshit."

"All right. I feel awful."

"We're not here to argue. If you want, we stay and talk, if you don't want, we get out. It's up to you."

"I want."

They spoke of their own addiction to alcohol, their complete loss of control once into it, the coming to realize it, and despite that, not being able to do anything about it, the worsening, the irreversibility, the prospect up the road, which was death. They knew it from the inside, and they were describing his own patterns, his own helplessness. But they were sober and clearheaded and even cheerful. They said they'd be back if he wanted. "Think it over." And when they left, he was alone. With himself.

He and nothing else. He had been stripped, no, that was putting it on somebody else, no, no, somehow he had become stripped—of everything. He had no friends, no money, no place, no work, no clothes, unless they'd washed the filth from them. A johnny shirt in some kind of hospital. That's what it came to. This, after the soaring happiness of drugs. He'd had it made. For the first while. He and Del. Deeper and deeper into that desert, the ego having its way, a mirage of lushness, green with promise. All gone now, into some kind of nothing. He felt picked clean, bones drying in the dusty wind, the glare fearsome. All was clear in that sky-blue room, sharpened by pain, a clarity with a price, no excuses, no rationalizations, no place to hide. Just himself, open, more than that, exposed, to elements he could not know.

He wondered if death were like that. The self he thought he knew was just not there. A strange awareness, as if mirrors had stopped working. The self he took for granted because he was busy responding to pleasure or sights or dreams or big ideas of what he was—all that was by the way and now no more. He was discovering, like expecting bottom and finding none, that he did not, could not, know himself. At best he was something, someone, who could be aware, and somehow could know other things, but not the heart of his own person. That was in existence by a different warrant. That was given. His to accept, to choose, to do, however weakly. And if given, oh, possible, if given, is this the desert where you meet the giver?

The dryer had stopped. He heard, then listened to, the buzzing of the fluorescents. Time to be with time again. The shock of that first experience had worn off soon enough, but the experience itself kept returning. It was there while he was detoxifying and withdrawing and staying sober, and he kept accepting it and came to understand that he was touching on something real. It was never without some twinge of fear, like a child swinging too high, and also never without a hint of freedom and even, at brief moments, of joy. But you don't live there.

He gathered up the dry clothes into the garbage bag, and took it to the wagon. Up the street near the main entrance to the supermarket was an outdoor phone booth. He went to it. The book gave him a main number in Sherbrooke, none for Ashton, so he got the operator and dropped in the amount she said. After two rings a woman answered.

"Alcoholics Anonymous, may I help you?"

"I'm calling from Ashton. There's nothing in the phone book. Is there a group here?"

"Ashton"—she was looking up something—"Ashton, yes, there is."

"Lemme have the number, will you?"

She gave it to him and he thanked her. He didn't pause, more coin, more dialing, four then five rings.

"Hello," a woman said. It was somebody's house.

"Is this AA?"

"Yes. Yes, it is. But Cliff's not here now."

"That's all right. I just want to know if there's a meeting somewhere."

"Oh, yes, he's at one now."

"You know where it is?"

"They use the hall over the post office."

"That the one on Township?"

"That's it, it's the only one."

"Okay, thanks a lot."

"Oh, you're welcome."

He wondered about her. She sounded as if these things still surprised her. The constant emergency of living. He felt better doing something. It had been weeks now since he'd made contact.

4

❦

"Hello, Pauline. I'm Claudia Poole. I've been trying to reach you."

It was evening, near eight. Del was sitting at the kitchen table, listening, slightly fearful of Mrs. Poole's boldness.

". . . Yes, it's about work in a way. I have a girl staying with me who does the same kind of work you do."

For some reason Del got ready to be embarrassed, as though she'd be called to the phone like a little girl to say hello.

"No, I'm not trying to organize a team, but it is an idea, isn't it? . . . There *is* safety in numbers. . . . Well, I'd like to talk to you in person . . . Can we be alone? . . . Then maybe I can drive by and pick you up . . . Poole. Mrs. Claudia Poole . . . I'm on Station Street."

She called out the phone number and repeated it.

"Of course."

She hung up and said to Del. "She's going to call back. She's being cagey. I can't say I blame her."

"You didn't tell her very much."

"Apparently I didn't have to. She's keeping trouble well away from her. She doesn't want me there, and it's clear she can't leave the house at this time of night without a lot of explaining."

In a few minutes the phone rang. When things got going again, Mrs. Poole said in answer to something, "From a customer of yours . . . No, I don't have your address, just the phone number . . . Let's say a former customer . . . All right, a Mrs. Roussel . . . Yes. You see, my girl was also fired."

Del felt that she'd have to talk about it now, and on the phone, but she heard Mrs. Poole say: "How about tomorrow morning? . . . Nine's all right. How about in front of the hairdresser's on Main Street? L'Esthetique, that's right . . . A red compact wagon, a Chev."

With that done, Claudia Poole dialed the other number.

"Hello," she said cheerfully, "can I talk to Beatrice?"

And Del began to feel embarrassed all over again.

When the blond girl in the light sweater and short skirt looked at the car, walked past, and then came back, Del decided to speak to her. Mrs. Poole was in the car, she wanted Del to be the one to make contact.

"Hi, are you Pauline?"

The girl looked at Del carefully. She was in her late twenties, short and muscular, trim, with the developed buttocks of an athlete. She tried to look into the car.

"That's Mrs. Poole, I'm Del."

"You the one who was fired?"

"Yes."

"All right, what's going on?"

Mrs. Poole leaned over and spoke from the open passenger window. "Come on in and sit down."

"No."

"We'll attract attention standing on the sidewalk. Here, take the keys, if that'll help."

"It's okay. I don't want your keys."

She got in the front seat, Del sat in the back on the edge of the seat.

"What are you after?" Pauline asked.

"I'll tell you in a little while."

"Why not now?"

"Things aren't ready, we're waiting for somebody."

Pauline grabbed the door latch, ready to get out.

"Who?"

"You and Del weren't the only ones to get fired. Did you know that?"

"No."

"We're waiting for the third."

She arrived a few minutes later. She was tall, in her late twenties, with long legs and a full figure, in blue pants and a red jacket. She had lots of black hair that set off a handsome symmetrical face and made her skin look even whiter than it was.

"Beatrice?"

"Yes. Are you Mrs. Poole?"

"No, I'm Del."

"The girl?"

"I guess."

"You know what I mean."

"Yes."

"Who are they?"

Del identified everybody. She got into the back seat first. But Beatrice hesitated.

"Do you drive?" Mrs. Poole said.

"Yes," said Beatrice.

"Then you drive."

Mrs. Poole turned over the keys to Beatrice, who got behind the wheel. Mrs. Poole joined Del in the back seat.

"Pick a place where we can have coffee and talk."

"All right," said Beatrice.

"Does anybody mind if I pick it?" Pauline asked.

No one objected.

"Okay, make a U and head straight out."

Beatrice did that, and as they were riding, she asked Pauline, "Are you another girl?"

"You mean like you and Del?"

"That's what I mean."

"Yes."

"This is gonna take a lot of trusting. I don't know any of you."

"Neither do I."

After a while Beatrice said, "You know, I kinda believe you."

* * *

Pauline picked a motel on the edge of town that had a large restaurant. Inside they sat at a table in the far corner that had windows overlooking the highway. They ordered coffee. Mrs. Poole collected her keys and made light talk until they were served.

"Well," said Beatrice.

She and Pauline were now tense and apprehensive, Del was nervous. They all looked at Mrs. Poole and waited.

"I think," she said, "that what happened to Del also happened to you."

"We know that," Pauline said cautiously, "you said it on the phone, we all got canned."

"I mean what really happened to Del."

"Okay," said Beatrice, "so something happened to Del. That don't mean us."

"No, not just like that. But I have a feeling it does."

"Have all the feelings you want. Just leave us out."

"Del."

Del looked at Beatrice, then at Pauline. She could only guess, but if they'd had an episode like hers, they would have to keep quiet or face unmerited shame, or even misunderstanding at home, you never know.

"I answered their ad," Del said. "She wanted references because, as she said, the last two girls had stolen things of her husband's."

"Ha!" from Beatrice.

"She really believes that!" said Pauline, still incredulous.

"I thought it was a bit odd," Del continued, "two people, just like that—"

"Odd's not the half of it," said Beatrice.

"—but I had no way of checking. So I went there to work, a Friday. And, well, after lunch sometime he . . ."

They looked at her sympathetically.

"I don't know how to say this. He was there, in a dressing gown, saying things, then he threw it off, and stood there, not a thing on. And he was, you know, ready. And he wanted me to do things, and he was going to film it."

"Him and his goddam camera." That was Beatrice.

"So I took my baby and got out."

"Your baby?!" Beatrice almost yelled.

"Yes. I always take her to work."

"How old is she?"

"Just over a year."

"And he still . . . ?"

"He wanted to give her something to put her under."

"The son of a bitch."

That made everyone silent for a moment. And Del went on.

"Then when I called *her* and tried to get paid, she said I'd stolen video movies from him—"

"Oh, sure!" said Pauline.

"—and that that was my pay. After that, I lost the two customers I'd given as references. She'd called them to say I was stealing things. So then Mrs. Poole figured it's time to find out who the other two crooks were, that's you."

They didn't laugh, they nodded their understanding. Mrs. Poole patted Del's arm and looked at the others.

Beatrice needed no urging. "He took tape of me working," she said, "and showed it to me, kept telling me how wonderful I looked, too many clothes on and all that, and then there he was, just like you said, and he wanted me to work him over. I said no. Then he argued. Then he said he'd put the pictures of me with the pictures of his, of him ready in close-ups, and show them around. I got out. I didn't get paid either. Then she phoned, he got her to phone, I guess, to get me to go back. I didn't. She phoned again just the other night. He's loony."

"You figure he still has the tapes," Mrs. Poole said.

"A guy like that? He'd keep them, he'd claim I was posing for him."

In the lull that followed, their attention turned to Pauline. She took time thinking about it, obviously not wanting to speak.

"He had a thing on my behind," she said, and had to stop. It sounded so silly she could hardly keep from laughing. The others didn't laugh.

"And he took pictures of me, too. That's all he did the first time. Said the lights would help me work. I didn't catch on. When I went back a week later, he showed them, they weren't me, just me here." She patted her hip. "I was all bum. And he was all worked up. He wanted it, well, from the back, just to run it against me, he said. I cleared out as fast as I could. I wonder if he ever got anybody like that."

"I hope not," said Del. "I think he buys it."

They didn't want to stay on the matter. They fell silent.

"Well?" said Beatrice.

"I think," said Mrs. Poole, "if you're all willing, we can do something about this."

Website Renewal: www.acpl.info
Telephone Renewal: 421-1240

Total items checked out: 5

Due date: 12/23/2013 23:59
Type: BOOK
Title: The lieutenant
Barcode: 31833010066700

Due date: 12/23/2013 23:59
Type: BOOK
Title: Separate flights
Barcode: 31833007340760

Due date: 12/23/2013 23:59
Type: BOOK
Title: The times are never so bad : a ...
Barcode: 31833014270463

Due date: 12/23/2013 23:59
Type: BOOK
Title: Hidden in dreams : a novel
Barcode: 31833063398034

Due date: 12/23/2013 23:59
Type: BOOK
Title: A lot to make up for
Barcode: 31833020074024

Allen County Public Library

"Do what? We can't do anything. They'd laugh, that's what."

"We can have a chat with Evalynn Roussel."

"Oh, my gosh!" said Pauline. "We can't do that!"

Martin watched two weeks go by. May into June. There was lots to watch at that time of year. But it was worse than just being idle or merely waiting. You can stop being idle by doing something, however frivolous, and waiting always ends. But this he couldn't end. He was accepting convalescence like a man eager for vengeance, ready to jump into things on the least rumor of returning strength. It wasn't quite the right frame of mind.

Nothing was happening quickly, nothing would. It was a special kind of tedium. Hour by hour was going by. He could sense the very time. He knew by the feel and texture of the day what things would normally have been done in that time, the vigorous work of a morning, the feeling that he was on top of things or even a little ahead of them, the stopping for lunch, the follow-up in the afternoon, a little more slowly, enjoying the visible results of jobs done, things coming into being under his hand, wood cut and corded, fences repaired, windows glazed, the house painted, the lawns kept trim, the harvest brought in over weeks, always on some sort of incalculable schedule, for it didn't go by any man's clock. The time and rhythm of day and season. And years of meaning. He had to let it all slip by. Hour by hour. Idleness that wasn't idleness, waiting that wasn't waiting.

He stayed outdoors. It had a way of making thoughts different and feelings less noticeable. He strolled for a time, up and down the lane, into the garden, examining things, then sat on the porch in the sunlight looking at miles of countryside. For long periods, nothing happened. He had time to note the shadows that were edging to the north. He saw woodchucks feeding in the field behind the garden. The mailman stopped at his box and beeped the horn when he saw him. A newspaper, *The Hampton Journal*, named after the county, a few ads, no letters. Two cars went by, a half hour apart, ordinary four-doors with a single driver; no hand-waving, so he didn't know them. The milk truck crawled from farm to farm, disappearing in the hollows, its stainless-steel tank gleaming two miles away. He wasn't bored, not outdoors. He watched it all, not passively like a man at leisure, but more as if he were taking a break, intending all along to go back to work or at least not intending not to. His mind kept scheming for ways of doing things. And time moved on, as slowly as the shadows.

Lunch was routine and welcome, it had him doing something, indoors, where it was unwise to do nothing. He laid out what he needed, plates, utensils, pots, took the trouble to peel a large potato and cooked it in a pressure cooker, eggs in a fry pan, made tea, and set about eating slowly, without much appetite. He turned on the radio and after a few minutes he turned it off. It was unreal, too sure of itself. It was like listening to people pretend. He had grown used to silence and the natural sounds that entered it. When he finished the last of the tea, he cleaned up and put everything away.

It was a discipline of sorts. He'd got into it when his wife died, a necessity then to keep from sinking too low, to let grief fade, and to meet, later, the hollowness of being alone.

He went outside again, walked for a while, and came in to lie down. He didn't sleep. It was a matter of policy to rest, the doctor's policy, and he followed it without murmur. He let the day's problems drift by, the same ones, they were insoluble at present, and he abandoned once more the idea of using machinery like the tiller. It called for strength he didn't have. His range was walking—and sitting. He'd have to stick with that. He let go, too, of any catching up with the now late season. It couldn't be done, unless his neighbors helped, but he couldn't expect that, he didn't need the garden the way a farmer needs to have his cows milked or his haying done. It was an extra. He grew some things for others, sold some to the stores, put up enough to last the year. A convenience, not a necessity. Such it was, seen from the outside. But for him it was almost a way of life. It brought him close to things, and their source. His hands set his heart free. He had begun that way and discovered he had a surplus. He'd do without it if he had to, he could forgo the surplus. He was discovering the beginning.

When the doctor's time was up, a half hour, he got off the living-room couch, went into the kitchen and out, to the left, to the sheds and workshop. There among the tools and materials he looked for and found an old narrow-headed hoe with a normal four-foot handle. He hefted it the usual way and again by gripping it near the head, took it over to the workbench and clamped it in the vise. Not wanting to waste strength hand-sawing, he used the power saw to cut the handle some sixteen inches from the head. He put the saw and the cut-off portion on the bench, unclamped the shortened hoe and hefted it again to his satisfaction. It would work. Primitive, and ironic next to the equipment he had, but basic. He had soil, and seed, and plants ready to go, and himself.

On a balanced cart, with two large spoked wheels like a bicycle's, which made lugging things almost effortless, he put the hoe, a foam-rubber kneeling pad, some baling cord, pointed sticks, a trowel, and three trays of tomato plants he'd started in early March. He wheeled everything into the garden, following the main path, and stopped at an area he knew got lots of sun and was protected from the prevailing winds by a bank of overgrown rosebushes. Going slowly, holding back the normally swift gestures that would have got the job done in no time, he laid out a line with the cord and sticks; then, starting at one end, kneeling, he used the short hoe to clear weeds from a section roughly two feet by three. Always slowly, as if he were searching for something, not quite like a child dawdling. It had come to that. But it was getting done. When the strip was clear he dug a hollow with the trowel and set a plant in the earth. One plant in that vast garden. He all but laughed. He stopped awhile, cleared another short strip, and set out another plant. He did a third. On the fourth, the going got a little heavy. It was hot, near 2 p.m., daylight time, the one o'clock sun. He got the box he'd been using for the purpose and sat on it.

Four plants. Not much, but there they were. It had taken time, that's all, and some effort. He tried to think of it, not as a piece of work to be done with him knowing how much and how fast and how long it would take, but merely as something to do, like playing solitaire to while away an abnormal time. But he wasn't playing and he couldn't quite kid himself that he was. No, that wouldn't do. The fact was he simply couldn't have that big a garden. At best he'd get a fraction of it, limited to what he could weed and plant and weed again as it grew, and harvest when the time was right. And that wouldn't be much. The rate was those four plants. But it would be something. He'd have to see. And the way to see was on his knees with the short hoe.

He got into the slow rhythm of it and did four more plants and stopped thinking about how much and how fast. It still wasn't playing but it did keep his hands busy. The soil was soft and workable, it had been tilled and fed last fall and built up over the years. But what'll grow food will just as readily grow weeds, and they'd taken everywhere, even in the part he'd tilled a few weeks ago. The row he was forming was clean, the plants stood out against the fresh brown soil, but the row itself showed up the wild green cover around it. Ten plants. The sight of them urged him on, but he decided that at a dozen he'd quit. The fatigue might get to him later. He figured it was after three o'clock. He'd been at it some two hours. Plenty for the first real try.

As he was putting things in the cart he heard a car on the main road and only glanced at it. But it was going slow. And as the sound persisted he looked at it again. An old Dodge station wagon, nobody he knew, no passengers. It stopped at his mailbox, backed up a little, and swung into his driveway. A visitor. He watched the car pull up at the house. A young man got out and looked around as though wondering where to go.

"Over here."

He pushed the cart out of the garden and left it on the lawn.

"Mr. Lacey?"

"That's right."

"My name is Hagan. Stan Hagan."

Martin walked over to him and they shook hands on the lawn.

"Do you have a moment?" Stan asked.

"Sure. I got lots of time. But I'm going to spend it sitting. Over here."

He led the way to the veranda at the front of the house, took one rocker and waved a hand at the other one. It gave him a chance to look at Stan, the first good look, after which a person ceases to be a total stranger: city clothes, sports jacket and slacks, not new, at least a city way of wearing them, indefinable, late twenties or more, lots of hair but trimmed, a long thin face, straight nose, a firm mouth, a little strained, not ready to smile unless there was something to smile about, bluish-gray eyes quick with intelligence, calm in a reserved way, or tired, as if he really didn't care, or knew something, hard to tell, good hands, not a wise guy, or a salesman, not with that car, not a volunteer of some kind, he didn't have that I've-got-a-right look.

"What's on your mind?"

"I'm looking for work. I was asking around in Ashton, I'm living there, and I got to the hardware store on City Gardens, Foster's, and the man there said you might be needing somebody. He gave me your name and how to get here."

"Does Bernie—Mr. Foster—know you?"

"No. He asked a few questions, where I'd been and things like that. I gave him what references I had."

"I guess he figured you were okay."

"I don't know. He didn't say."

"What kind of work are you looking for?"

"Any kind. Unskilled, minimum wage, even less. I have the car."

They left the subject there, no pushing, no selling. A good few minutes went by.

"Bernie was only partly right. I can use help, no doubt about that, but I'm in no position to hire anybody. I can't afford wages."

"Part-time would do."

"I still can't afford it."

That seemed to be that. They fell silent again. It wasn't awkward, they simply weren't saying anything. Neither of them was in a hurry, there was nothing to be in a hurry about. It made time just another part of the scenery.

"I'm going to have some coffee. Would you like some?"

"All right. That'd be fine."

"Everything in it?"

"Whatever you're having."

The sun was at the side of the house toward the back, the veranda was in shade, and the shadow of the house and the trees which he couldn't see covered a large section of the lawn. The rest was in sunlight, bushes with mulch around them, to flower later he presumed, a hedge marking a perimeter, then the hay field as far as the road, the maples lining the driveway, and past all this wherever he looked sections of forest and rolling fields, natural and worked. He could see it, he felt, because he was doing nothing else, just looking at it sitting in the shade on a porch. Somehow the place looked trim, and wondering why, he realized there was no debris anywhere, no junk, nothing left hanging around, no extra chairs or clutter on the veranda. It was new for him, both the country and sitting this way, and he felt at ease, not as if he were resting but more as if he were being welcomed.

Martin came out with two mugs and gave one to Stan.

"Are you broke?"

"No, not quite. But it's coming. I've been living on what I saved."

"You lose your job?"

"Not exactly. I quit, to do something else, I work to finance what I'm doing. Right now I could use a job that'd pay the rent and leave me some free time."

"Are you a writer, or something like that, a student?"

"No."

"You're not married?"

"No."

"You're not from around here."

"No."

"Well, it's really none of my business, I was just making conversation, in a way."

"That's all right." Then after a while: "This is nice country. I've seen a fair amount of it, driving around. Do you farm?"

"No. I used to when I first got settled. I rent it out now. You ever done farm work?"

"No."

"You don't seem too worried. I mean, about finding work."

"I can always find work, I take anything. What I need is time, not money, but money buys it."

"Nothing buys it."

"Yeah. You've got a point. It goes. But it's always there, isn't it?"

"That takes finding out."

"I suppose it does."

"Those references you mentioned, the ones to Bernie . . ."

"People I worked for in Middleton and East Windsor, and places I lived. Do you want them?"

"No. They sound pretty recent."

"Yeah. The last few months."

"If I looked past them, would I find something?"

"Nothing spectacular, nothing somebody who knew the scene couldn't guess, the usual freedom, the usual misery, no prison, if that's what you're getting at."

"Just wondering."

"And no mental institutions."

"I didn't think so."

"If you looked, you'd find a blank. I've been drifting."

"College?"

"Yeah."

"You got relatives?"

"A sister somewhere, my parents are dead."

Silence once more. It was part of the conversation. They sat and looked out on the main road. Stan finished his coffee and put the mug on the rail of the veranda.

"Well," he said, "I guess I'll be on my way. Thanks for the coffee."

"A pleasure. I wish you luck. All I can offer is room and board. For part-time work, raising a garden crop. Anyway, the work's always there."

"I'll keep it in mind."

Martin watched him disappear around the side of the house, heard the car door close, the motor start noisily and reluctantly, and saw the old wagon backing down the driveway. Stan hadn't seen the turnaround past the sheds and didn't turn on the lawn. City all right. He swung onto the road to face Ashton, honked, waved, and drove off.

A trail of dust arose as if trying to follow the car, but it blew to one side and settled softly. A silence returned, made evident by the sparrows and robins and grackles, the silence of having been with someone, and soon the silence of being alone. Talk never reaches down there, it takes place on another level. There was something silent about the young man. Not secretive, silent. He had talked openly, revealed little, would have talked more if questioned, but sparingly, in a way silently. And about what? Not just hard luck or not having a job, that seemed to be incidental. This wasn't the Depression, that was fifty years ago. Fifty. No, something closer than bad luck, something inside. The usual misery was how he put it, he had a name for it. Life gets to you early now, being young doesn't seem to have a meaning. No joy to one's youth. Down a dusty road in an old car that can't make it much longer. And being old? He gazed at that for a while: being old is being now, no difference, not inside, save realization, the road was always there, dusty or not, the way. And meaning.

It was time to start deciding what to make for supper.

Stan felt as if he'd left something undone, or worse, done something wrongly. The talk with Martin was fresh in his mind, now in snatches, questions and answers, a little filler here and there, not much though, a touch of irony, or was it humor? Nothing he could analyze. His feeling didn't seem to be about what was actually said. There was something else. But he had to let it go and pay attention to the unfamiliar road. Farms on both sides, bush and fences and fields, some for pasture, some for crops, it was no wilderness, it was somebody's property, all surveyed and properly mapped and recorded in the county offices, the roads were all side roads, the equivalent of city blocks but miles apart and far from square, a wrong turn and you drive for twenty minutes before you get to a sign that makes sense.

If he was right, he was looking for a T intersection and he was driving toward the top stroke. A native uses names, take the Labelle Road and get to the Madden place, a stranger uses the alphabet and a little geometry, X, Y, T, somewhere in a rectangle, only it's never that neat. The conversation kept coming back and kept eluding analysis. It wasn't in the content. It wasn't a matter of pinning down a job, that was all clear and all irrelevant in a way. Maybe there was nothing to look for, just a mood, a remembered atmosphere about the old man.

The road curved and came to the T. He turned right, into more curves and downhill, shifted down to spare the brakes, and a mile or so later when things flattened out he arrived at the paved highway and turned left for Ashton. There was traffic, easy traffic, some of it fast, just people finishing work and getting home, which couldn't be far, the routine of a small town, small by big-city standards, dull too, if you believed the stuff on television, but beautiful to him, at least human in scale, though he wasn't really part of it. Strange that you have to have nothing to see something.

He got to Mill Street and made an early supper as fast as possible without scurrying, hot dogs and leftover salad and milk, and drove out to the Lennox place. He had returned to see them, at first in case they remembered anything about Del or anyone else who might help, and later because he knew them somewhat and dropping in was better than aimless reading or watching TV or sitting around getting depressed. They and Kay Saunders had become involved and could gossip with people Stan could never meet. But that was all it yielded, local gossip. He wanted to see Lennox early, before supper, when he could make it short without offense and while Lennox was still sober.

He wasn't. They met outside and stayed out, perhaps to avoid Mrs. Lennox.

When he got around to it, Lennox said: "I met Mike Donly, who works at the co-op and gets election work when a campaign's on. So we get to talking and I says, any chance you got some of those electoral lists hanging around, I'd like to look somebody up. So he says yes and we keep talking and I buy him a few and we finally go over to his office at the co-op where he keeps his stuff, he can't do it at home, not enough room and too many kids digging into everything, you know, a man's got to have a place to keep things. So he let me have the lists and I ran down every line, twice, and no Symons at all. Course the list was last year's, they'll be updating it soon, but that doesn't help us out, now does it?"

"No, it—"

Lennox kept going, "So then I went back to the pub where I knew Lucien Daigle'd be dropping in. He runs a store on Township Street, a general store, not much of a place now that things got specialized, but he's made his money and it gives him something to do. And he's got help in the afternoon, not that he needs it, Marthe Bienvenue, she likes to work part-time to get out of the house and do things—"

"Was she of any—?"

"—and she practically runs the place, the ordering, the books, doing new things, you know, competing and making money. He kinda lost heart when things changed. Anyway, his daughter works over at the unemployment and I put the word to him and he didn't want to go directly to his daughter so he got Marthe to do it indirectly, if you get what I mean, and she gave the daughter some story about bills not being paid and all that, a very natural cover, and could she look up this name to see if the person has been getting any benefits. Well, a snap, just looking up the records . . ."

"And?"

"Nothing. No Symons."

"Well, thanks for—"

"So. She pulled the same thing, Marthe I mean, with the welfare people, but that took some doing, because I'm told the person over there, I forget his name, kinda likes to protect people from bill collectors, so when Marthe caught on she switched her tune fast and said that if the girl was on welfare she'd write off the bill, and the guy, I wish I could remember his name, Lucien knows of course, but it's not important, the guy looks it up and again there's no Symons, not on welfare."

"Thanks all the same, that's a lot of good work."

"Just conversing around, easy enough. I got to thinking, who'd be able to check at a glance, so to speak, instead of going around asking a lot of questions and making a big thing—"

"Yeah, right. Well, I've got to—"

"—and getting everybody curious, people are awful curious, if they see you buying a shirt they begin wondering what for and what might be coming up that they don't know about and then they want to know about it, so they start talking it up and pretty soon everybody knows and there's a story going around about why you want to get dressed up. Indirect's the best way, so when I met Mike Donly I figured I'd chew a little fat with him. . . ."

Stan tried and failed to interrupt. Lennox repeated his news as if he hadn't done it already. He expanded his observations and added more of his views on life and it didn't stop until Mrs. Lennox called him in for supper. Stan brought the car over to Kay Saunders's place.

The inside main door was open, for him to enter, he knew, but he tapped on the aluminum screen door. He had barely touched it when the old lady called out.

"Come on right in."

She was in the tiny kitchen, having supper, sitting at a swing-up table at the side window. She had a view of the Lennox home. She waved him to a chair opposite her.

"Have you had supper?"

"Yes, I have."

"Will you have some tea?"

"When you're ready, don't interrupt your supper."

"I'm finished."

She put her dishes in the sink, also tiny, ran water on them, and got busy setting up two cups of tea.

"I see he was telling you."

"He sure was." Then to soften the remark, "He's all right."

"He told me, too."

Stan couldn't help grinning at that.

"The first time was in the morning and he made it

short, she's not a voter, not on unemployment, not on welfare. The second time, the same day, was just before the ball game and I got the whole thing. The ball game took him inside. He sits there all evening, drinking beer, grumbling. Too bad. As you say, he's all right, which makes it a shame. I'm glad I live alone."

"He might get fed up with it one of these days."

"No. He's already fed up. He's got nothing. You work all your life, and you've built nothing. Production, for the company. They got the lib movement wrong, they forgot to free the men. I can just see it"—she burst out laughing—"thousands, no, millions of screaming women stopping the whole economy yelling: Give our men their balls back!"

And she laughed all the more, helplessly, as though enjoying one of life's great impossibilities. Stan grinned, and smiled, and finally laughed at this delicate old lady's abrupt realism.

"Maybe you should organize," he said.

"My husband was a union man, I've had plenty."

When it all subsided, she sipped some tea.

"My news is no better," she said. "She hasn't gone to any of the health clinics, here or in the other towns, not for herself and not for the child. I checked with the volunteers, easy enough, they talk to me. And you?"

"Nothing."

"I guessed that."

"Meaning?"

"You're here. You're not the kind to just drop in, you need a reason for visiting people."

"I suppose. I've covered about everything. I'm pretty

sure she's not working in this town, at least not at anything public."

"Would she know you if she saw you?"

"You mean, fast enough to duck?"

"Something like that."

"I don't think so. Not just a quick look. I'm a lot different, in appearance, I mean. It was . . . well, different. And I haven't passed her over accidentally, I'm not looking casually, and I've thought of her, of how she'd look if this or that were changed. You know."

"Hair mainly."

"That's about it, or glasses."

"So what's next?"

"More of the same. I guess. I'm not sure she's *not* around. Just a feeling."

He stood up and thanked her for the tea. She seemed a little disappointed that he wasn't staying longer.

"Do you go at this full-time?"

"More or less. I'm also looking for work."

"Oh, God, how often I've heard that."

"I'll bet."

"Well, keep in touch. Or at least . . ."

When she didn't continue, he put in, "At least?"

"If it all comes to nothing, at least drop around to say goodbye."

"All right, I'll do that."

He got into the wagon and was about to turn on the ignition when he felt once more that something had not been done right. This time it was clearer: I could have stayed, he told himself, and talked, just talked, or listened, it wouldn't have cost a thing, a little time, a little less self-concern, I'm in no hurry, she's not just an informant, and the old man was not just a guy hiring somebody. It felt too late to go back, the moment had passed. She had hinted, no, everything else had hinted but not her, she was too knowing to make demands, that never works anyway, and too powerless to initiate anything. The marginal old. Like the marginal young. Do it. He took the key from the steering post, went back to the screen door and tapped on it.

"We didn't," he said when she appeared, "finish all the tea."

He was back in Ashton a little before nine. It was dark, the twilit sky barely visible beyond the streetlights. He was looking for a phone booth.

He was glad he had talked with Kay Saunders. It was the sort of thing he should have done sooner. She had a lot of stories about labor unions, more about her children, all of it real to her, but only of passing interest to him. He had told her nothing. What mattered lay elsewhere, in the simple fact of visiting for a few hours. He was learning, he let it go at that.

He found a booth on the toilet side of a gas station. The place was closed, the office lit by a bright fluorescent which spilled light into the booth. He looked up the old man's number.

"Mr. Lacey?"

"Yes."

"Stan Hagan. I was over to see you this afternoon."

"Yes, I recognize your voice."

"All right if I come round in a few days?"

"Anytime. I'll be here."

"I mean, to work."

"That's what I thought you meant."

That was settled. He felt relieved. He was beginning to feel conspicuous in town. Being at Lacey's would solve that. He didn't want a fringe job with long hours, he'd had those, they were meant to get him this far. It was bad enough as it is without going another round with small-town cheapskates.

At the Mill Street place he got the landlady and explained that he'd be leaving.

"You took it by the week, you know."

"Yeah, I know." He wasn't going to argue for a day or two's rebate. "It probably needs cleaning."

"They usually do."

"I'll be out in a few days."

"That's fine. Leave the key on the table. Remember, whenever you're in town, this is the place."

It sounded like a slogan her late husband had made up.

"Yeah, I'll remember."

The fake motel room was depressing. He was fine, of course. It was the room.

5

❦

The biggest EvaLynn store was in a shopping center off Main Street on the west side of Ashton. It was prominent, across the walkway left of the main entrance, with some fifty feet of glass, the usual store-long name across the top, mannequins lit by spots, recessed lights inside, and everywhere large bright sales tags bearing the store's logo. It was quiet, near eleven on a Thursday morning. The only customers were a few unhurried middle-aged women looking closely at the tags.

Del and Mrs. Poole went directly to the cash register, where a smartly dressed woman in her thirties seemed to be in charge.

"Are you Margaret?" asked Mrs. Poole.

"Yes, I am," she said with a pleasant routine smile.

"Mrs. Roussel is expecting me. Claudia Poole."

"In the corridor"—she indicated the back of the store—"to the left, the second and last door."

"Thank you."

The door was open. Mrs. Poole tapped on it. "Mrs. Roussel."

She looked up and took a moment to place Mrs. Poole. "Come in."

She was at the first of two desks along the wall on the right. The unoccupied desk had a computer on it. On the far wall were four low filing cabinets heaped with papers and fabric samples. The rest of the room had a trim sofa that could sit three, comfortable chairs with armrests, scattered as though a meeting had broken up, a narrow table along the corridor wall, and on each wall prints of ladies in elegant nineteenth-century styles.

Mrs. Poole went in, followed by Del. And it was then that Mrs. Roussel noticed her.

"Oh," she said, "are you—?"

"She's with me."

"Aren't you—?"

"My name is Del. I worked at your house."

"Yes, you did." She turned to Mrs. Poole. "You said you were bringing somebody with you. Is this the one?"

"There are others, they'll be here. We have to talk a little first."

"If you wish. But"—she glanced at Del—"it's a rather delicate subject."

"It certainly is."

"Perhaps it would be better if you and I—"

"I don't think so."

Sensing something, Mrs. Roussel kept them standing while she stayed seated. She put her elbows on the surface of the desk and played with a pen as she thought things over. Then she sat back and looked at Del.

"I gave you two names the other day." She addressed Mrs. Poole but kept looking at Del. "Hers wasn't one of them."

"No."

"Did the others give you her name?"

"No."

That got her attention. She stared at Mrs. Poole. "Then how did you make contact?"

"I didn't. You see, Del lives at my place."

"She does, uh?" She looked from one to the other as she thought it over. "That puts a different twist on things. I'm afraid there's something I don't understand."

"There is. May we sit down?"

"Not unless it's necessary. If you're preparing for some sort of legal action, you can see my—"

"No, it's not that."

"It's got to be something like that. If it's about an accusation of pilfering . . ."

"There was no pilfering."

"But she—"

"There never was any, ever."

"Sit down."

Mrs. Poole brought a chair from the far wall and placed it within range of the desk. Del moved the one next to the sofa. They didn't sit down. At Mrs. Poole's direction they set up two more chairs.

"I'll get the others," she said. And before Mrs. Roussel could say anything she was into the corridor and on her way to the front of the store.

Del took the innermost chair, to the right of the desk, and together they watched the open door. Mrs. Poole returned almost immediately, followed by the two women.

"This is—"

"I know who they are."

She placed Pauline in the chair next to Del, Beatrice in the next one, and herself last, to Mrs. Roussel's left. The two women were visibly ill at ease. They looked mainly at Del and Mrs. Poole, glancingly at Mrs. Roussel.

Her face had gone blank, she had the look of a person steeled for the worst.

"It's hard to talk about these things," Mrs. Poole began, but Mrs. Roussel waved a hand to stop her.

"I take it," she said, taking in the three young women, "that none of you stole anything from my house."

"No." "That's right." "No."

"Then my husband must have been mistaken."

"Three times," Del said, "three different times."

"And what does that mean?"

"It wasn't just a mistake," said Beatrice in a low voice, "he made it up."

"You're saying he lied."

"That's what I'm saying."

"Why would he do that?"

"To cover up the other thing."

"What other thing?"

The three looked at each other and at Mrs. Poole.

She in turn looked at Del, who finally said: "His sexual advances."

Mrs. Roussel looked Del up and down, then Pauline, then Beatrice, hair, face, figure, legs. She did it fast, her eyes darting to and fro, trying in vain to solve something.

"That's vague," she said. "How can you be sure?"

"I'm sure."

"I'll need more than that. I'll need detail."

"Perhaps," Mrs. Poole said, "you'd prefer to talk about it one on one, we could—"

"No. Here. And now. In detail."

They told her. First Del, then Pauline, then Beatrice. At first she looked at them straight on, and gradually she turned away and kept staring at the open door. When they were done, she was crying, holding a Kleenex to her eyes, unable to speak. She waved them out softly, pleadingly.

In the parking lot, Beatrice said: "I'm kinda sorry I did it."

"So am I," said Del. Pauline nodded.

"We all are," said Mrs. Poole.

She pulled open the door to the drugstore and held it with one foot as she pushed the stroller through. She felt safer inside. The baby gawked at everything and uttered sounds and made pointing gestures which Del seemed able to interpret. The woman at the counter, severe-looking in a white coat, with glasses on a small chain, said "Hell-lo!" to the baby and got a reaction and repeated it a few times just for fun. From a container suspended from the back of the stroller Del took out a small poster. It was a little bigger than typing paper, ten by twelve inches, made on a computer, and looked professional.

"It's about the Fashion Fair . . ."

"Oh, yes."

"Mrs. Poole, the lady who organizes it . . ."

"I know her, she's just over on Station Street."

"Yes. Well, she asked me to ask you if I could put it up in your window. Is that all right?"

"Sure it is. Give it to me, I'll put it up myself."

She took it from Del quickly and efficiently, and immediately got busy with a roll of invisible tape. She didn't want anyone messing with her window.

"I always go to that fair."

In no time the poster was up. Del thanked her and the baby made her palms go bye-bye. Del backed out of the front door, pulled the stroller through, and headed for the next likely place on Township Street.

She was careful on the sidewalk. She had left the house by the back, checked the street and the railroad station for anything other than trucks. The only thing she could look out for was a pale blue car. If he used another one, she wouldn't know until too late. She had hurried down the driveway and walked away from the house as fast as she could. She felt silly doing it. The baby thought that going fast was fun and squeaked for more. On Township she had begun on the far side, going north, and planned to come back on the other side, always facing the oncoming traffic.

She wasn't in her work clothes. She was in a blouse and skirt, not everyday wear but something to dress up in. Her hair was done, Claudia Poole had insisted on that, and paid for it, Del's appearance was part of the advertising. But she had held out for flat shoes, it was going to be a lot of walking. She was wearing sunglasses. It was a sunny June morning, a Monday, one of her lost workdays, the fourth day after they'd seen Evalynn Roussel.

They had heard nothing. All they could do was let time go by. It wasn't even waiting. No one could know anything. No one got in touch with anyone. That one time had been enough, it made the meeting possible and it was over. There was no follow-up even for curiosity's sake, it wasn't that kind of arrangement. Del and Claudia Poole didn't talk about it. Claudia said that talk can make some things worse, and this was one of them: talking was a way of worrying. As it was, they both knew that something was going to happen, or was happening, or wasn't, and that they wouldn't know about it until well after the event, and then by accident, if at all. Even waiting, if you did it, was worrisome. So Claudia had put Del to work.

The glasses, and the clothes, and the hairdo made her feel disguised, unrecognizable except by someone who knew her well, and that was no one if you didn't count Mrs. Poole. She was a stranger on a strange street. In a strange town, too, if you came right down to it. What could give her away was the stroller, and, of course, the baby. She had an identity there. The child knew her. And she felt they could spot her through her child. They? No, not they, him. With that idea came a twinge of panic. Quickly she looked at it: no, he'd be looking for a girl with a stroller, all right, but a girl in jeans, any girl would do. That, too, was a sort of identity, being known like that by him. It felt like a curse.

She was to cover the places where women would shop, and by the look of it, that was nearly everywhere. It was simple to skip the others: the barbershop, a haberdashery, the poolroom, a mechanic's. She did a shoe store, a yarn shop, a restaurant, a women's clothing store, a gift shop. People were nice to her, women fussed over the baby. Many, once reminded, seemed to know about the fair, it happened every spring. Most people didn't know about Claudia Poole, though, and Del found that fascinating: some things just aren't public, she too would remain anonymous, virtually unseen, unremembered. Nobody asked her about herself, she was just someone handing out advertising. She passed over the hotel, they'd be transients.

The post office, where she was allowed to hang a poster from the lower rim of a bulletin board, ended the businesses on that side of the street. She crossed Township and started back south. At the supermarket, after waiting for the manager and explaining how many people were expected at the fair, she was able to tape a poster on the glass to the right of the main entrance. At the Laundromat she put one in the window and one inside, so people waiting could see it. Farther down the street, she stopped outside the bar-disco and wondered if many of its customers were women. Two girls, still in their teens, in makeup and tight short skirts, dancers most likely, came out and saw Del looking at the photographs of the shows. They noticed the baby.

"Hi," Del said.

"Hi," said one, "you looking for work?"

"Not here," said the other, "not with stretch marks."

"No," Del said, "I'm putting these up, for the fair."

She took out a poster and showed it to them. The baby waved her arms at it, and the first girl waved back and made noises at her.

"Any good?" asked the second girl.

"Very good," Del said, reminding herself of Claudia, "the knits are all handcrafted, cost you a bundle at a boutique. Some of it's right out of *Vogue*."

"Oh, yeah?" said the first girl. "Can I have one of these?"

"Sure." Del gave her the poster.

They were beginning to attract attention. Men driving by took long looks at them. The girls took it for granted.

"Can I have one, too?"

Del gave her one, too.

"I'll put it up inside."

"Thanks," Del said.

As she started on her way, the first girl said, "Say, hon, are you married?"

"No."

"You must work hard."

"I do all right."

"I bet you do. You wanna get yourself a little something?"

"No," said Del. "Bye."

"Bye." They said it together. The baby waved at them.

She noticed a few cars gawking at her, but as she got farther from the club she blended back into the Monday-morning pedestrians. She did a few more places, a beauty parlor, a jeweler's, a Sear's outlet, another restaurant. She lingered a little more, tended to the baby inside, talked a little longer. She felt more and more uneasy on the street. But she completed Township Street.

Then she went back to a street north of Station, along that for almost a block until she was at a gravel lane which took her to Station a little past Poole's. Once there, she hurried to the driveway and up to the back of the house. Only then did she feel relieved.

When she was getting lunch ready, alone, the phone rang.

"Is that Del?"

"Yes, it is."

"This is Mrs. Davis."

"Oh, yes."

"I shouldn't have let you go. I'm sorry. It seems there was some mistake. Do you think you could work for me again?"

"I think so, Mrs. Davis."

"Mondays?"

"Yes."

"Thank you, Del, thank you."

"That's all right."

And later that day, before supper, as Del was finishing with Betty and Claudia was preparing broccoli for a quiche, Mrs. Melling called with a similar apology and offer. Del accepted. She turned to Claudia, somewhat pale.

"She really did something. That poor woman. Evalynn Roussel, I mean."

"I know."

"I guess I'd better call the others."

"They'd want to know."

She did, and they both said the same thing: "He's gonna be mad."

"I'll show you where you can put that."

Martin noticed that Stan didn't have much luggage, two canvas pieces and a plastic suit bag, but he didn't say anything. He led the way from the kitchen through a dining room of sorts and into a large living room that was the entire front of the house. To their left against the wall ran a banistered staircase. He let Stan go first and followed slowly. They went into a long room at the back of the house. It had a dormer window on its long side where the ceiling sloped and an ordinary window on the narrow side overlooking the sheds. It was country, as seen in pictures, but it was new to Stan.

"This is the west side, you won't have the sun waking you up at five in the morning."

Stan put his stuff on the bed. "That's a thought."

Downstairs, from the wagon, Stan brought in a supermarket paper bag and put it on the kitchen table.

"The remains of groceries. I cleaned out the fridge where I was staying."

"Let me buy that from you, then we can start out even. You can eat anything you want any time at all."

"I'll donate it. That makes us just as even."

"It does at that."

Martin lifted out a milk carton, less than half full, some bread, and a hunk of butter still in the original wrapper. He put these in the fridge. The rest, a few cans, all unopened, he left on the table. Little enough to leave alone. He felt he was poking into someone's life.

He led Stan outside to the sheds and showed him the workshop and the equipment. At first Stan thought he was being put right to work and he felt himself becoming the employee: alien, a little unreal, his time suspended by someone else's will, ready to perform actions that wouldn't be his. But Martin kept pointing things out and explaining what they were, moving on slowly as if they had nothing else to do. Obviously he wasn't setting up any jobs. Stan went along with it, much as a visitor would, and wondered as a matter of curiosity, not worry, if anything was up.

Martin examined the tractor and stared at it as if trying to make up his mind. He hadn't used it in weeks, now months. Running it didn't take that much effort unless you had to keep shifting or twisting around to watch what a plow was doing.

"Ever been on one of these?"

"No."

"Hasn't been used for a while. It needs a little exercise."

Martin climbed into the seat, started the engine on three cranks, waited for it to warm up, and moved the tractor out of the shed. As it idled, he got off to show Stan how to ride the back of it, where to put his feet, what to hold on to. Then he got back up, made sure

Stan was perched correctly, and set off across the field behind the house. Second gear low, about as fast as walking. Stan had no trouble holding on. The noise of the motor made conversation difficult.

At the far edge of the field they passed through a border of hemlock, ducking branches as they did, and got into a rising woods of beech and maple. All Stan saw was big trees spaced at random, nameless to him, growing in uncountable numbers. The ground was a mulch of rotting leaves, no grass, with patches of sunlight here and there and a scattering of tiny flowers, blue and white, looking somewhat out of place. Martin guided the tractor along a wheel-rutted trail that never went straight for long but seemed to be the only direction to follow.

When the rise leveled off, they came to a clearing that had several big piles of chopped wood, mounds of slash, and stumps where trees had stood. Here Martin stopped, turned off the engine, and they got down. The stillness let them hear things, a crunching underfoot, surprisingly loud at first, clothes rustling, birds chattering somewhere. Martin looked at the piles of wood as if they shouldn't be there.

"That looks like a lot."

"About twenty cords, short cords. I cut it last winter. I haven't been able to get it in. Maybe by the fall."

It didn't seem to occur to him that he had help. He looked around without saying anything else and got back on the tractor.

They continued along the trail. It took them over another long rise, meandered to the left, and stayed roughly parallel with a barbed-wire fence. Martin followed it for quite a distance, inspecting it for breaks as they went by, and turned, again to the left, downhill this time and into lower, soggy ground. There were cedars here, no maples, and no trail. It felt as if they were riding through the evergreens, slipping and churning in a sort of mossy mud. Eventually they got on firmer ground among regular trees and on the trail once more. Stan didn't recognize anything until they were pushing aside hemlock branches and emerging into the field.

The house and the buildings looked small in the distance, a quarter mile or so, roofs, sidings, the trees compressed above them like bushes, the whole thing standing alone on what seemed like a vast plain, made even vaster by the sky. A look was enough to take it all in, a glance could pass over it. It wasn't like seeing it from a car or a train, it stayed put, it was a place they were going to. The effect lessened as they got closer, and vanished entirely before they got there, as if it had never happened. Martin put the tractor back in the shed. It made it seem they had merely gone for a ride.

Stan couldn't help asking: "When do I start working?"

Martin laughed. "You already have," he said. "I must admit I wouldn't have gone on that tour alone."

That made it sound mysterious, so he added: "I'm still recuperating, from the hospital."

"Oh."

"Besides, you're not dressed for it."

"These aren't my good clothes."

"They're wrong for the job."

"I'll have to get some secondhand."

"No need, there's lots here."

He led him to the shed adjoining the kitchen. It was long and wide, a two-story addition, with stairs against the long wall, the studding exposed, the wood unpainted, all of it clean. It had the remains of the winter's firewood at the far end, in the middle things stored seasonally, and against the kitchen side on a row of hooks clothes of all sorts, overalls, denim jackets, work pants, footgear on the floor. It served as a changing room.

"There's something there that'll fit you, pants, shirts, they're all clean, even belts if you look, and work shoes. I'll go get you some socks. Then I'll show you some work."

They began in the garden.

"You know anything about this?"

"No."

Martin explained the need for loose, well-fed soil, the north-south rows for maximum sunlight, a layout to make weeding easier later on when things got crowded. In the workshop he showed Stan how the tiller functioned, had him go through the steps of starting, running, backing, stopping, especially stopping, and in the garden he demonstrated how it all worked. Then he left Stan alone with it.

"Go ahead and do it wrong," he said. "It'll show you how to do it right."

Stan played with it, he could hardly do anything else, until the machine grew less monstrous and more obedient to what he wanted. He held on grimly to the handlebars, walking in his own tracks, and left large deep bootprints in the tilled soil, not at all like the smooth strip Martin had made. Eventually he got the hang of it and was able to walk at the side of the tiller and guide it by using only one handlebar. He started afresh, redid the early rows, and became fascinated as, strip by strip, a vast smooth garden bed was taking shape.

As the work went on, it required less effort and less attention. And when he stopped to look things over, he became more and more aware that he was outdoors, in the sun, wearing a hat at Martin's insistence, alone on this quarter acre, alone also in the surrounding farmland and the hills and the horizon on all sides. The newness was strangeness, despite the peaceful beauty of it, and the strangeness wasn't a distraction, it was another nowhere—the same, it seemed, as all his other recent experiences. Except for the work. Somehow that was closer to being real.

At lunchtime he scrubbed his hands clean and offered to help.

"Oh, you can watch, you'll get to know where things are."

They had eggs and potatoes, panfried reheats—as Martin pointed out it was quicker that way—bread, butter, milk, a meal more elaborate and substantial than Stan was used to. There was something to talk about: tilling. He now had pertinent questions to ask, and Martin answered them, amused at the impracticality of verbalizing it, ending invariably with "I'll show you." Stan did the dishes as soon as they were finished eating, and they went out to the front porch for coffee. Nobody was clocking a lunch hour. But Stan wanted to be doing something.

"You've done a good piece."

"Well, I'll do some more. It's the kind of thing that should get done."

"It'll wait for you. It's not like harvesting."

"It's all right. I want to do it."

"When that thing runs out of gas, let it cool off about fifteen minutes, then we'll fill it."

"That's called taking a break, eh?"

Martin laughed. "Yeah. And it prevents fires."

He gassed it twice throughout the afternoon. And, apart from those needed stops, he kept the machine going. With each pass he made the bed that much wider, the untilled area smaller, and when that grew visibly less he couldn't let go. It was that kind of work, something growing under his hand, the results there to see: perhaps a quarter of a football field of fresh soil. The tiller, he'd found out from Martin, moved a half mile an hour in low gear and made a swath a little less than two feet wide. And as he worked he calculated that in theory he would be traveling some five thousand linear feet, more with overlaps, a mile of garden. A meaningless calculation. It had them laughing when he mentioned it. "Drive you nuts," Martin said. Stan had noticed him trying to hoe the tilled soil into mounded rows. He did about ten feet and had to stop. After that, from time to time, he went around the edges, marking off where the rows would be. It was near five when they put things away, changed, washed, and set about organizing something to eat.

In the kitchen, things were different. In the outdoors the work had been leisurely, arduous in its way, but also enjoyable. Here it was a little like an emergency. It wasn't hurried, but it was non-stop, Martin didn't dwell over anything. By the time Stan had peeled enough potatoes, Martin had the pressure cooker waiting for them, the ring under it red-hot. And in the dozen or so minutes it took to cook them, two fry pans were ready to cook the steaks, a steamer was doing frozen peas, the table was set, plates stood ready to be served, and an electric kettle was already heating water for tea.

No fuss, no time wasted, no extra motion. And no talk that didn't deal with what they were doing. Stan could sense something of what was going on, he lived that way himself. Without that kind of discipline, he wouldn't have eaten at all, not alone, and not in a kitchen. Hungry and tired, he would have been drinking. It was a lot faster. He wondered about Martin.

But when it was all ready and they sat down to it, Martin was back to taking his time. It was as if a minor crisis had passed. Stan was surprised at how good the food was.

"Last year's stuff. It's kind of old now."

"It's still different."

Martin laughed a little at Stan's reaction. "That's what they all say. It's the peas. Meat and potatoes people are used to, that's standard. But stuff frozen right after it's picked, that's usually new. It can't be done on a big scale, so you don't find it in the stores."

"I wouldn't have known to look."

"That's the way it goes. It can be served up a lot

better, too. Cooking's not my game. My wife was good at it. Herbs, that sort of thing. Takes time, and feel. And you have to have people around. I just get it warm and eat it."

They could have been talking about car repairs, the food didn't really matter. It was the absences. The discipline that filled in for something more natural. There was no dessert, except for cookies, which Martin remembered and Stan refused.

They did the dishes, quickly and efficiently. Stan said no to Martin's weak invitation to watch the TV news, noticed in passing the three bookcases in the living room, and they went and sat on the porch with mugs of tea.

The outside seemed tranquil now, it wasn't summoning them to work. It was early evening after a long day. The birds were busy and sometimes noisy. In the distance, too far to see fences, a herd of cows formed an intelligent line from barn to pasture. Nothing passed on the main road and it looked as if nothing would. Even the noises were quiet, heard just as they were, no background to overcome. Things seemed to have a place. And time.

"It's good to have that done," Martin said. He could see a section of the garden from where they were. "You've been a big help."

"I enjoyed doing it. It's . . . well, it's different."

"I hope you didn't overdo it, the first day."

"It doesn't matter. I wanted to get tired, physically tired."

"That's a sure way to do it."

"I guess it is."

"What I'm getting at is that it's going way beyond earning your keep. I don't want to take advantage of your circumstances . . ."

"I know you don't. It's all right."

"If you're keeping track of it . . ."

"I'm not."

Martin couldn't help laughing at the inverse haggling.

"All right. What I meant to say was, you're storing up a lot of keep as far as I'm concerned. It's important to get a thing like that straight."

"Yeah. I know that. I want to play fair, too, Mr. Lacey . . ."

"You can call me Martin."

"No, I prefer Mr. Lacey."

"Fine with me."

"You see, it's possible I won't be staying long. It all depends. I'm . . . I'm just waiting something out. And I don't mind what I do in the meantime, as long as it's doing something."

"Okay. You know your own affair."

"I wish I did."

"Oh. Well, if there's anything I can do . . ."

"No, I don't think so. It's not anything that specific, it's just life, mine, and where it is right now."

They left it at that.

There was something about the room. It was noticeable enough to catch his attention. The sloping ceiling, for one thing. It began about halfway across and met the outer wall some three feet off the floor. It made the room a sort of lair, a place you could sleep in, and it laid out, as if by a gesture, where you could stand and sit and lie down. The head of the bed was at the low end of the slope, where else? and along that wall was a chest of drawers, a bookcase, a small table, an armchair near the dormer window. It was a room in somebody's home, furnished as life had gone on, not something made over to be rented. It was years since he'd been in one, and never with a sloping roof. He was too tired not to be at ease, but that's all it was, ease, nothing more lasting. He was in another strange room, a new place he happened to like, but not—what? Home? Home went with boyhood. Your father's house. Not much of a ring to that, he rented. No mortgage, no grass to cut, no painting, just images from movies and ads. Your mother's house maybe. You couldn't say that for long without having somebody laugh. Something had made all that meaningless. But it hadn't removed a longing.

It was dark out, the dark just outside the windows, light pressed back into the room, miles away a small yard light, people the old man would know, no need to pull the shades except against the morning light. He was by himself, but not alone in the house, and that changed the kind of thoughts he had. It made them less tenacious, less demanding to be resolved. Did it take so little? Or was it so little? The presence of another, who accepted, without questions, without pressure, who took time and, more, who kept peace. Was not a little of the longing met? Rare, almost never, and always temporary, found, as if by accident, and, if sought, lost. He to me, his home, house, his peace.

And what, who, would meet it, even as an echo in the heart, for the old guy? No, not the old guy, make it Mr. Lacey, you were right the first time, don't betray him with language, it's too easy. Who?

Big brown bugs the size of his thumb knocked on the windows, once, and buzzed and fluttered on the screens. He put out the light, got to his knees without trying to say anything, and got into bed as if he weighed a couple of tons. The bugs went away. The ringing in his head turned out to be some kind of chirping from outside that sounded like a million crickets. Surely it couldn't be that. He'd have to ask. He sank into bed solidly as if he were lying on the earth itself. Gravity could go no farther.

Martin expected him to sleep in, but Stan was up early, he'd set his alarm. Better up, even if only half awake, and aching, sipping coffee, it made the day seem less defeating. Martin insisted, by simply making it, that they have a good breakfast, and by seven they were outside in the soft sunlight, dew still on the ground, the air warming fast, birds everywhere. They took things slowly, with little talk.

From the sheds they took the tools and materials they needed, hoes, stakes, baling cord, a small sledge-hammer, a six-foot one-by-two grooved at intervals, gloves, and wheeled it all to one end of the long central path. Just off the path, in the newly tilled section, Martin drove in a stake, then another near the fence some twenty-five feet away, and tied baling cord between them just off the ground. Using the one-by-two as a spacer, he had Stan drive in two more stakes some five feet away from the first set, strung the cord, and set up a third set. With these in place, he showed Stan how to hoe the soil into mounded rows. "You can bury the cord, it doesn't matter, it'll come out easy."

As Stan hoed, Martin set up a few more stakes, and when the first row was mounded he removed the cord and the stakes and put them aside for later. The idea of staking ahead was to stay out of each other's way, but the system, if pushed, would suggest hurry by laying out all the work to be done. If you're alone, any system would do, but this way the pressure was on the man doing the hoeing. So Martin dropped the staking, and when Stan finished the next row, he stalled and chatted, and did that until the system disappeared, and from then on as each row got done they had to stop and take time to mark off the next one.

Stan thought Martin had gotten tired, and when they were taking a break, on the porch, he said: "I'll stake a few rows ahead, it'll speed things up."

Martin laughed. "All right. If you want it that way. But I can do that."

"You sure?"

"Oh, yes, I'm sure."

Stan let the work, and the day, define itself. It got slow and dull, repetitious, exacting in its own way, no skimping or getting too careless, not if you wanted a real mound that went straight. The tedium ended with each row and it could be relieved at any time, all he had to do was stop and look around and lean on the hoe and talk. He took frequent breaks in the afternoon when the sun got hot, and Martin came out only to move the stakes. The monotony was quieting. It wasn't aimless, it had a purpose, for now and later, which he could appreciate, but it wasn't his. Strength and young manhood were his, and little more. You have to be innocent to have more.

After supper, and the dishes, he went out to the bare garden and looked at what had been done. The paths were well trampled, the rows undisturbed, the once fresh earth now dry and paler. The results of his efforts were all there to see. It wasn't a job. He had made something. He was tempted to do more, the tools were still out, but he had changed from his work clothes. It would keep. He made his way to the front of the house and joined Martin.

The porch was becoming the place to sit after working for a time or all day. It just fell in with things and it took on a tone, not of relief merely, but of completion. To be there came to mean that something had been accomplished. They didn't mention it, it was simply felt and understood, shared by being known. Tired by that kind of work and resting that way was worth any number of drinks. Still you thought of it, that track was always there. And the switch. The low sun was making the rows in the garden stand out.

"That's starting to look like something," Stan said.

"Yeah, freshly made like that. Later it gets all green, of course, looks as if you never touched it."

"It's a lot of work."

"You're trying to do it in one crack."

"I mean the whole thing, for one man."

"Takes me two, three weeks. This time, though, I was going to let a lot of it go. Just till it, keep it in shape for next year."

"Do you have to mound it like that?"

"No. But it's better if you do."

He explained about drainage for heavy rains, root systems, exposing more soil to the sun, easier weeding. It was know-how and experience and it made sense. To Stan it was an old man who knew a lot more than he could do.

"It seems kinda big to me."

"Yeah. I guess it is. That's just the way it turned out. There used to be people around here. We all worked at it. My wife was the gardener. Little by little, that all changed and, well, the garden didn't. It gives me a lot to do, and that's important when you're alone."

"You're making it sound simple."

"That part of it is. What's not so simple is learning how to do nothing."

"Yeah. That I know something about."

"You might at that."

"It's really more than being alone, isn't it? That just makes you more aware of it."

"It?"

"The rest of it. There's a big difference. No net, no lifeline, just you. Even that."

"Yes. There's degrees of it, I guess. Depends on what you had before, what you were, how much you can let go of."

"Or have to let go of."

"Yes, that's harder. You're kinda young to have come to that, if we're talking about the same thing."

"Today that's how it goes. Young doesn't mean anything."

"Yeah, I guess that's true."

"What I'm talking about is . . . having everything come to nothing. And I mean everything, all of it."

"That about says it, if anything can. You're not just making philosophy, are you?"

"No, I've been there."

"How can you be sure?"

"Sure of what?"

"Sure that you'd come up to the edge of nothing."

"There was nothing left of me, Mr. Lacey, except me. And even that I can't recognize."

In the quiet that followed, Martin said: "They used to call it—dying to one's self."

"I've heard it used. It's true."

"It's not a matter for therapy."

"No, I found that out."

More silence for a long time. They seemed to be watching the twilight dimming.

"I can use some coffee," Stan said, and got up.

"Help yourself."

"Make you some tea?"

"Sure."

When he came back with two mugs, they drank without speaking. The moment was still with them.

"It was fast with me," Stan finally said. "That's what young does. Sudden, if a few years can be sudden. At twelve I was an alcoholic, I know that now. Later I was into drugs, deep. And sloppy, I was too far gone to steal right. So I got back into booze, it's cheaper and legal, no hassles, no pushing, but it was just as sloppy.

So I went all the way down, and wound up in a clinic, a real zero. I didn't even have my body to call my own. And . . . two guys from AA turned up, I had called for somebody, it seems, so I was wishing for something deep down, and I—tried. That was a year and a half ago, nearly two, I have to think back every time to be sure."

Martin just listened.

"Everything went. It had to go. It was all tied in with ego and the habit and all the rest of it. So then it was me, pretty small, a fragile something, that's the way one guy put it, but something, cold sober, trying to find reality in all that nothing. Scary. It still scares me. You see, there's no going back to normal, normal is another illusion."

"So's that nothing."

"Yeah, but it's strong."

"It's always there." Martin waited, and said: "And now?"

"You mean?"

"You're not just wandering around."

"No." After a while he continued. "I'm trying to find a girl that was with me back then. I put a lot of my misery on her. Hell, it was more than that, I almost killed her. I want to try to set some of that right. It's one of the steps in AA. A hard one. None of them are easy."

"She out here?"

He told him of his search for Del.

After that, they didn't try to make conversation. It was time to leave it alone. The night took on its form of light, the driveway was discernible, the trees all black against a starlit sky, the glow of a town, probably Ashton, on the horizon, yard lights too far away to make a difference.

Stan got up and took the mugs.

Martin went ahead. "I'll get the light."

As he was about to go upstairs, Stan said: "Those brown bugs that bang on the windows, big things . . . ?"

"June bugs."

"And all that chirping outside, like crickets, all over the place?"

"Those are frogs."

Nice to know something.

The work in the next two days was routine for Martin, except that this time he was supplying little but know-how, and he couldn't help thinking about their conversation. It put everything on a different level, beyond social protocol, and it explained a few things he had felt about Stan, his reticence, his evident detachment from the normal young-man things, the discipline that was still conscious. It also raised yet more questions which he didn't, and wouldn't, ask. More wonder than questions, even a sort of worry, it goes with being an old father. He knew that Stan had risked something in speaking. Easy to shatter a person's insides. It was one thing to open up to a fellow AA, quite another to go into it with a stranger, an old man at that who might be too stiff to accept it, let alone understand, an employer in effect, though the job wasn't crucial, who would think him unreliable. Employer. The very idea made Martin laugh. Meat and potatoes for wages, and a bed that wasn't being used anyway. For labor that simply couldn't be bought, labor that few could deliver. There was pain behind it. And ahead of it. He wished he could do something.

For Stan it wasn't routine, it was all new. He finished the mounding, and in the remaining flat areas he tilled furrows for corn and potatoes. He learned how to sow seed and how to set the young plants Martin had started indoors, he carted compost and aged manure and water where it was needed, he drove in posts with a ten-pound mallet and they strung chicken wire and old page wire for climbing plants like peas and pole beans. Each phase seemed precise enough because Martin knew what he was doing, but the whole thing looked rough, though orderly, just long mounds of earth, bare except for the transplants, on which nothing seemed to be happening. Yet it was all there, growing and ready to grow. Between them they'd shaped every cubic inch of it. It had a satisfaction of its own.

On the following day, a Saturday, after coffee, when they would have started working again, Martin said: "Do you have anything you want to do?"

"Yeah, I have. I want to check out the wagon. I'd like to go into town."

"Fine. You see, Stan, the work is over, what I had in mind when you first turned up. So that puts things on another footing. Let's just say you're not working here anymore, you're living here."

"That's what I've been doing, Mr. Lacey."

"All right."

"I'd still like something to do."

"Oh, there's lots of that. But it can wait for when we're good and ready."

"Okay."

Stan went outside, a little uncertainly, Martin imagined, or was it that a presumption established over four, five days, long enough, was being violated? He ran hot water over the breakfast dishes and scrubbed them quickly and thoroughly. He felt more humanly in place, a repose of sorts, something had settled, or could settle. There were no artificial roles to play, one who hires, one who works, definition by pay, he had removed them, consciously, always a risk if the human is not already there. Only the deeper ones remained, old and young, country, nature, but these had a basis, a reality, they need not be roles.

He could hear Stan's old Dodge. It was grinding out a few labored cranks, each weaker than the other, hardly enough to get anything going. Finally it, or Stan, gave up. Martin was almost elated. He laughed inwardly, knew he was grinning outwardly. Things were back to normal—breakdown: typical of country living.

He went out. Stan had the hood up, in dismay, yes, that fit, and they stood looking at the car the way men do, as if the right pronouncement might solve things.

"Battery's down."

"We'll get it inside, you can work on it there."

Martin got the tractor out and backed it to the rear of the wagon so that its drawbar could be connected to the car's hitch. With Stan in the car to steer it, he pushed the wagon up the driveway, stopped just past the sheds, pulled it into a turn to line it up with the garage, and maneuvered it inside. Stan unhitched the vehicles and Martin got the tractor out of the way.

Inside, they got to work. They put water in the battery and set it on a 10-amp charger. It would take time. Martin started a small compressor, and while that was building up pressure, they got to the air filter, which needed cleaning, and exposed the choke mechanism and its linkages, all dirty, and inspected as much of the engine as they could without taking things apart. When the compressor was ready, they cleaned the air filter, sprayed solvent on the linkages and blew them clean, put air in the tires. They added a quart of oil, put fluid in the windshield-washer tank, and looked for anything else that could be fixed. They were like a couple of teenagers trying to tune up a bargain, except that they weren't dreaming, they knew the absurdity of an old car. Most of the morning went by, and to save time while the charger was still going, they had lunch around eleven.

Near noon, they went back to it. Martin disconnected the charger, left the cover off the air filter so he could see what was happening, and Stan got in the car and turned the key. The engine caught, smoke and spray shooting up past the choke, but it ran. They both laughed. Martin flushed carburetor cleaner down the choke, watched the exhaust go black and clear up, and finally closed everything. Stan backed the car out of the garage, swung it to face the main road, let it run awhile, and turned it off. Half a day had gone by, the sort of thing you do on vacation.

Stan washed and changed. They divided the domestic chores. Stan to do the laundry in town, Martin the shopping. Martin gave him coins and bills.

"The expenses are mine."

"I don't want to make you short."

"That's okay. You won't. I can go long periods with very little money. I'm well provisioned, you're not."

"Yeah. Smart."

"No, just old. It often looks like the same thing. Get some oil and a filter."

He led him to the kitchen porch and pointed, where the rafters met the horizontal, at what looked like a fistful of dried mud and discolored straw.

"An old bird's nest. I leave a key in there."

6

❦

Around two o'clock, Del was touring the displays for Claudia, to see if anyone needed anything. This section of the fair was in the high-school gym; another was in the school yard, to keep the kids occupied; and another in various classrooms, where instructions could be had on how to make some of the things on display. She had the baby with her, in the stroller, now fed and asleep. And as she lined up with the open gym doors she could see the people in the corridor beyond, and among them Evalynn Roussel. She had watched for her earlier and had given up, and was now taken by surprise. Del went to one side and stood unmoving, getting ready to be seen but hoping not to.

Evalynn was in a black-and-white sleeveless blouse and a red skirt. She had a large handbag strapped over her left shoulder, it was open and heavy, a small clipboard stuck out of it. She was wearing tinted glasses. She looked quickly at the displays around the three walls, took in the crowd, saw the young models on the three raised platforms at the fourth wall, and decided to go in that direction. Three panels of judges sat at long tables in a roped-off area in front of the platforms. Near the edge of the outside platforms, two girls at microphones announced each appearance. There was music in the background, not rock, and people were active and noisy. They were taking pictures of everything.

Del watched Evalynn walk behind the judges' tables and stop to look at the models on the stages. She turned the stroller slowly, not to waken the baby, and dodged her way across the floor to the knit-wear display. She put the stroller against the wall and sat behind one of the tables. The three women in charge of the display, which was Claudia Poole's specialty, were busy answering questions and making sure no one but themselves handled the clothes. They paid no attention to her. Del had been Claudia's general helper all day, and she was now invisibly part of the fair. A young girl, one of the volunteer models, still flushed after the stage fright of appearing in public, brought back one of the knits, a fall outfit.

"It's so exciting," she said with squealing emphasis.

The older women smiled at her.

"You gonna win?" Del asked. There was a contest for best model.

"Oh, gee!" And she went back toward the platforms.

Del felt old.

Through the crowd for an instant she caught sight

of the black-and-white sleeveless blouse, the glistening dark hair above the pale skin, the tinted glasses. Evalynn seemed to be taking in the displays. Del lost her for a while, then saw her again trying to peer above the crowd—she seemed to be looking for a particular table. Then the tinted glasses found and held on Del. Evalynn went behind the displays and came toward Del along the gym wall.

"Hello, Del."

She took off the glasses and put them in the handbag.

"Hello, M—"

"Please, it's Evalynn."

Del got to her feet so they wouldn't have to talk over the noise. They stood near the stroller, they looked like two friends doing nothing.

"Evalynn."

"I want to apologize. I'm sorry I thought badly of you."

"You had to believe somebody."

"Still, it was damaging to your reputation, you have every right to sue."

"Sue? I didn't even think of that. Besides, I got my customers back, you must have cleared me with them. Thank you."

"It was the least I could do. Here. Unfinished business."

She took an envelope from her handbag and gave it to Del. It wasn't sealed. Del looked inside. It contained a check for $42.50.

"I'd make it more if I thought you'd accept it."

"No. This is fine. It's what you owe me."

Del gently lifted her purse from the foot of the stroller and put the envelope away.

Evalynn had her glasses in her right hand, ready, it seemed, to end the conversation and put them on. But she simply held them, probably for something to do, and with a visible effort she managed to say: "Did you—does anyone else know about this?"

"No."

"You didn't tell anyone?" That was more like her old self.

"No. It's not the sort of thing you want other people to know."

"The other two girls?"

"Even less, they have husbands most likely."

"I haven't told anyone either, *anyone*."

"About the three of us, you mean? Getting together?"

"That's right."

"How did you . . . ?" She couldn't bring herself to say it.

"The tapes."

"Oh. Yes."

Evalynn put the glasses back in her handbag. She looked at Del steadily and a little incredulously. "Thank you," she said and went by the table into the crowd.

Del sat down. She felt sad about the whole thing. She had wanted to know more about what Evalynn had done, but she hadn't been able to ask. They hadn't been exchanging confidences, it was still business. And maybe a little honor—self-respect anyway. At the hint of tears she tried to take an interest in what was happening at the tables. She looked at the women talking to the volunteers and noticed someone at the side of the last table, a short blond girl with the stance of an athlete: it was Pauline.

Pauline caught her eye once, looked away immediately, and began to wander the length of the three tables toward Del. When she was close enough to be heard, she still didn't look at Del. She pretended to examine the display and said quite clearly: "He's here."

Del looked nowhere.

"The washroom," Pauline said and walked away.

"All right."

The baby was awake. Del set the stroller so that Betty could sit up and see things and wheeled it slowly through the crowd and out the open gym doors. In the hall, past an engraved plaque—Ashton High School Athletic Complex—that was surrounded by pictures and names, she found the girls' washroom and got the stroller through the doors. Pauline was near the sinks. Beatrice was in front of a cubicle as if ready to run in and hide. She was taller than the swing door on the stall.

"He's here," Pauline repeated, like someone announcing defeat.

"With that camera," said Beatrice.

"He was over where the girls are modeling," Pauline said, "*and* behind there, the locker rooms, where they're changing."

"Somebody said he was doing it for the EvaLynn chain and the big companies. They think it's great, they're gonna be seen by professionals." Beatrice couldn't contain her scorn. "A professional jerk, that's what. The son of a bitch."

"He better not see us together," said Pauline. "Or even alone. If she put it to him, that is. He's gonna want to get even."

"No," said Del, "it's not like that."

"What do you mean?"

"Well, just after she paid me, we talked a little—did she also pay you?"

They both said yes.

"—she said she left us out of it."

"Completely?"

"How could she do that?" asked Beatrice.

"She said she used the tapes."

"Oh, gosh," said Pauline. "Yes."

"And what happened then?" Beatrice wanted to know.

"She didn't say."

"He don't know we turned him up?"

"Apparently not."

"So he's not out to get us."

"Not yet."

"I'm still staying out of his way."

"Maybe he doesn't remember our faces," said Pauline.

"Then we better wear blankets," Beatrice quipped and called him a few more names.

"All right then?" asked Del.

"Okay." Pauline looked at Beatrice, who nodded. "Let's not leave together, he's got a nose for places like this. I'll get the door for you."

When she got back to the gym, she saw that Claudia

Poole had seen her from the display tables and was coming over to her.

"There you are," said Claudia. "I thought you might've gone home."

"No, just to the washroom. But I'm thinking of it."

One of the girl announcers exclaimed that a Lindy Masson was the winner of the Fairest Model contest and Lindy stepped forward from the line of girls on the platforms. Amid the applause and camera flashes, Del noticed a chubby man with thinning hair, a bald spot showing from the back, his face pressed against the viewfinder, aiming a camcorder at the girls. Mr. Roussel, of course. Others had smaller versions. One man in his thirties was taking stills with a square camera, which he cranked speedily. He looked like a man at work, a real professional, he had another camera dangling from his neck. Del wondered about photographers.

"Oh, stay," said Claudia. "Our display won a prize. I'd like you to share it with me."

"Be glad to."

"They might even take our picture." There was mischief in her eyes. A little satire, against everybody.

Del laughed. She wondered if Claudia had seen him. She must have, she missed very little.

To hell with him. But she thought of Beatrice, and the blanket.

·

Martin put the bag of groceries on the floor of the pickup. The boy who had followed him out of the store, wobbling under a box too big for him, let it drop on the passenger's seat and darted back, apparently unaware of Martin's thank-you. They never waited around for tips. Maybe it was because they knew most of the customers. Strangers tip. Martin laid the bag on its side, it would have fallen over anyway, and rocked the box a little to make sure it wouldn't. He got in and waited awhile before starting, he was tired and feeling it. It was a little after four. He drove away slowly.

He left Township for Main, going right, stayed on it for a few blocks and turned into a side street and parked. From there he walked to the side entrance of an old stone-and-brick church and went in. He was early, as he often was. He nodded at someone he knew by sight, and took a seat, glad to have time, he had looked forward to it, and let himself become aware.

It was a simple act, presence, acknowledged, he was in the way of not struggling over it, a turn of awareness, a steering close to existence, let what is be. No formed words, no framed thoughts, these were asides, surfacing as they will, time later for thinking about them. Here, with presence, he could just be, strongly, clearly, as he could with no other person, not even with himself in ordinary circumstances. More and more of late. Always fleeting, not to be maintained, sometimes as sharp and sudden as shock. And always he let it alone.

Seventy dollars' worth of groceries, $71.29 to be exact, in green electronic figures, you can't get more existential than that. The girl's flying fingers beeping out numbers, everything made precise, coded, translated into money, another fantasy. Making something into nothing, the real is rare enough without that. They've got me, I'm a family man again, there's comedy there somewhere, fixing old cars, worrying. I'm all the society he has, no, not society, community, society changes, it's all figured out, if you need something, you're a market. He, young, lives like an old man. On less. $71.29. Food is silent growth somewhere, life to life, not precise, not that way, not green numbers, you might as well get precise about hunger. Another lost metaphor. What have we done? Hunger, longing, oh, what that is.

"The Lord be with you."

"And also with you."

The priest was in his forties, graying a little, with a lean face that looked ready to smile. He was intent on what he was doing, as if he had given it a lot of thought. He'd have had to, it wasn't that easy. Martin had grown to trust him. A young girl in a pretty yellow dress, of high-school age Martin surmised, did the readings, careful to enunciate properly, the memory of thousands of years survived her rendering. The priest read from the Gospel and spoke of it, briefly, remindingly, and soon after was into the heart of what he was doing. He took bread, and wine, and words not his.

Martin watched and listened. For him the actions being done and what they meant had taken on a clarity he could only look upon: too physical to be simplified any further, too factual to be altered, free of any fantasy. "Before he was given up to death, a death he freely accepted . . ." Seeing, hearing, presence asserted, done, now there. He was aware of his belief, aware that it was belief, faith, as given as existence, as inexpressible as anything else that lives inside, real to the point of making all else real. I am with you. Always.

"The body of Christ."

"Yes."

Silence, echoing with other silences, brief, and gone. Let it be, don't reach, you can be sure of him. What's conscious is yours, and he is more than what you're knowing. A time to be, just be, it'll do.

The garden's in. It's made. I never thought it would be, I had let go of it. Another thing to slip away, a good thing, small of course, but big for me, what better than earth and living things and work that acknowledges creation. And that, too, slipped away, good as it is. It is only as good as it is, something on the way, you have to pass it to get further, closer, free of lost baggage, hurt as it may to lose. And then it was back, with a youth and energy not mine, back surely not for me, I had let it go, not mine at all, returned, found, still foregone, my lost luggage serving—isn't that it?—serving as luggage for someone else on his way. Oh, that young, young man, pained, paining, to make your heart break, I ask for him. I ask. Him and my not found son, baggage I will never surrender. Ask.

"Go in peace."

He left a little behind the others, people talking, voices very clear, car doors slamming, engines starting with a gush of power. It would soon be quiet, nothing around the building. The second car behind the pickup was an old Dodge wagon, Stan's, and he was beside it, waiting. He came over almost shyly.

"I saw your truck," he said, "then I saw you inside."

Martin sensed he was being told something. "I was early," he said.

"I should've realized, I guess. I'm still new at it."

"You can't know things like that."

"Nobody talks much about it, do they?"

"No. We've lost the words. A lot of talk, about how to feel good, no words."

"It's all desert, isn't it, Mr. Lacey?"

"You could say that."

"And one well."

"Those are very old words."

"Not for me."

Martin opened the door of the pickup. "Next time we can use one car."

They laughed.

"The guy who spoke about it," Stan was saying, "didn't speak about it, not directly."

It was raining, a straight light rain in warm air, summer settling in. They were on the porch, something of a habit now, and it was Monday, early evening. It could have been no time at all. Their ease had a hint of comedy about it, not entirely unfelt, the two of them in rockers, just sitting, a distance from each other, facing out, like a couple of hicks in a movie.

"His name was Daner, Gerry Daner, in AA, he's a priest, he's in his fifties. I'm not breaking confidentiality, you'll never meet him, he's on the Coast, and he wouldn't care if you knew. He was into science, philosophy, a university career, a big know-it-all prof, he called himself, he chucked it all to go back to what he started out to be. Thank God I'm a drunk, he said, and broken, or I'd still think I was virtuous and knew things and could tell others all about themselves, imagine. I can hear him, and see him, smoking one cigarette after another, drinking coffee, laughing away as if he'd played a dirty trick on himself.

"One time, a bad time for me, early in the game, we got to talking about it, trying to talk about it, a higher power, God, and he said to me, we can't know—and he really came down on that word, "know"—we can't *know*, not the way we think knowing is knowing, he's too different for that, we have to believe. And, I said, maybe a little too casually, what do I do to believe? And he looked at me and started crying, my question got to him somehow, just tears rolling down his cheeks, no sobs, you have to understand that that kind of experience, I mean all of it, is pretty moving, emotional, and he said: Ask. And later I did ask. And much, *much* later, I began to see."

Martin kept quiet.

"And later, not to see."

"So I asked again. And again. It's like that." He stopped, groping his way toward what he was trying to say. "Not so much up and down, like feelings, but a blank, then not a blank, mostly blanks, and a lot of thinking. Then it dawned on me that when you're asking, really asking, you're asking someone. You can take it that he's simply there, and that asking is always possible."

As he heard what he said, he waved it away and added: "I know that can sound silly, a projection, the sort of thing . . ."

"Why not? It's human. You're not gonna change that."

"Not likely, eh?"

They stopped talking, sidetracked, and waited.

"That man, on Saturday," Martin said, "the priest, he said once that at times, not always, but at times, the prayer you're making will change you as you're making it. That comes from way down. It's a kind of rough test."

"Yeah. That's happened, especially at first, when you've been standing in your own way." Then out of more silence: "But somehow, with him there, and you there, asking doesn't seem as important as just knowing it's so."

Martin said nothing to that. It was a subject of fewer and fewer words.

Stan blew out a lungful of air as though frustrated. "We're still not really talking about it," he said, "are we?"

"No, not really. But it's there. You see, we wouldn't even have something not to really talk about if we didn't believe."

Stan started laughing, absurdly, like a man who'd been struggling with an unlocked door. And the more he turned the idea over, the more he laughed.

"A paradox," he said. "Three negatives. Gerry Daner'd laugh and yell, a paradox!"

"That's educated talk."

"It sure is. What's it in plain talk?"

"Just the laughing. It'll do fine. That's what comes first anyway."

The phone was ringing. They finally heard it over their noise, and Martin went in to get it.

"It's for you."

Stan got to the phone. It was Kay Saunders. She didn't identify herself, she just started right in.

"You get newspapers out there?"

Stan grinned. She had thought he was crazy to live on a farm.

"Oh, yeah."

"*The Hampton Journal* likely, it's the only one."

"Yeah."

"Well, today's edition, the weekend social stuff, inside, I only got to looking at it now, page 6, you'll see a picture and a story about a fair last Saturday. She's in the picture, one of the prizewinners. You got that?"

"Yeah. I'll take a look. Thanks a lot."

"You can thank me by letting me know, soon."

"I will."

He told Martin, who got the paper and spread it on the kitchen table.

In the upper right was a two-column picture, three inches deep, of a group of women standing on some kind of platform. Over it in three columns, WIN AT FASHION FAIR, and under it a cutline of names, Mrs. this and that, and the fourth name, A. Symons, followed by more. She was the youngest face in the group, which enabled him to pick her out, but he didn't recognize her. For some reason she had sunglasses on.

"Could be," he muttered, "could be."

The story said nothing about her, no address, no town.

The masthead informed him that one Richard W. Holling edited the paper at 36 Main Street, Middleton.

* * *

He got there around nine. He was wearing a jacket, proper slacks, and a tie.

The building was two stories, red brick and wood, with four tall windows on the bottom floor topped by rounded arches. Small-town Roman, full of atmosphere. The windows on either side of one entrance bore the letters THE HAMPTON JOURNAL, also arched. The other entrance was a discount shoe store.

Inside was a long wide corridor on the right, a polished wooden railing on the left, a swing gate straight ahead, desks and table behind these, and four people, two men and two women, fairly young, busy over a lot of paper. He went through the swing gate, spoke to a girl at a desk, and waited while she went somewhere in the corridor. The others didn't even look at him.

"In there, to the right."

The man in the office could have been in his forties. He was chubby, wore glasses, had lots of brown curly hair, a bushy mustache, and dark stolid eyes as expressionless as the rest of his face.

"Mr. Holling?"

"Hm-hm."

Stan showed him the paper at page 6.

"I've been trying to reach one of the women in this picture, Adele Symons, the fourth one, here."

"Hmn."

"This is the first indication I've had about where she might be."

"So?"

"Well, I thought I could find out a little more about her, her address if you have it, or one of the people in charge of the fair."

"You're not a relative, that much is clear. Are you a collector?"

"No, nothing like that. I'm a friend."

"From way back, uh?"

"Yes, as a matter of fact."

"Pretty far back, I'd say."

"Go ahead and say it."

Holling snorted at that. He seemed to be acting. "What do you want to reach her for?"

"Just to see her."

"How long have you been looking?"

"Lately. I only just heard that she was around."

"She from around here?"

"Could be. Are you digging for a story?"

"Ha!"

"Well, Mr. Holling . . . ?"

"All I know's what's in the paper. The stuff comes in, every year, picture and all, we do a rewrite, mainly deletions, and that's all."

"And you don't know who sends it in, is that it?"

Holling shrugged and spread out his hands.

"You're stalling me, of course," Stan said.

"What if I am?"

"So why not come right out and say so?"

"All right, I'm saying so. I don't know you. I don't want to give you any information. I don't want to be instrumental in supplying some kook with what he thinks he needs. Is that saying so enough?"

"Yeah, but too late."

"Too late for what?"

"Nothing you could figure out."

In the car he took off his tie and put it on the seat. He made a U-turn on Main Street and got out of Middleton going over the speed limit and still getting nowhere with the complacent Mr. Holling. Not a relative, oh no. A small-town wise guy. Deletions they are, eh? Cuts will do, Mr. Holling, cuts. A Big Professional. It's a wonder he didn't call in the cops. Hey, I've got a guy here asking about a girl, a girl's picture in fact, it doesn't take much these days, first time it's ever happened, oh, he's calm enough, now. A few miles of that and he pulled in at a french-fry stand and walked around the car counting the wheels. All right, so he didn't tell you, he put you down instead. So? The hell with him. There's other ways of finding out. Back on the road he let the scene replay itself whenever it came up, fading a little each time. No resentments, remember? All right.

He kept going through Ashton on 131 toward Elizabethville, took the turnoff that put him on the parallel dirt road, and went to Kay Saunders's place.

"Something went wrong," she said when she saw him.

"Does it show that much?"

"Never mind that. What happened?"

"The editor clammed up."

She wanted the details, so he gave her what sounded like a complete account. But she had questions anyway. She made coffee while they were talking, and got out the newspaper and handed him the phone book.

"Bringley," she said, checking the cutline, "Mrs. F."

He found an F. Bringley, called out the number, and she dialed, got someone and went into her act. All about the great success the fair was, such a nice picture, how she couldn't make it, how she usually looks up the prizewinners, boutiques, buying, prices going up, and so on until she was able to hang up.

"She doesn't know the others."

The second name yielded nothing. The third one had her looking intently at the paper, then listening impatiently, a talker, and doodling, but finally it ended.

"A Claudia Poole, right here."

She put her finger on the picture, the second person from the right.

"What about her?"

"Adele Symons lives at Claudia Poole's. They won jointly. How do you like that?"

"Just fine" was all he could say.

He looked up Poole, C., and reached for the phone. She stopped him like someone flagging down a car.

"A man'll get nowhere asking after a woman."

He called out the number and she dialed.

"Hello, is Adele in? . . . Any way I can reach her there? . . . Oh. Will she be in later, this evening? . . . Okay, thanks, I might try her then."

She hung up, a little puzzled.

"Mrs. Poole, that was her, I gather, doesn't know where Adele is working, or won't say. Isn't that peculiar?"

"I guess it is. But she lives there. 18 Station Road.

Right here in Ashton. You sure did it. Thanks a lot."

"I was busting to do something like this last night. But I minded my own business. I shouldn't have."

"That's all right. It gave me a chance to meet Mr. Holling."

He decided against phoning first.

He had gone back to the farm, told Martin what had happened, and got busy for the rest of the day. They hauled firewood from the bush and he corded it in the shed nearest the house. He hadn't been able to stop thinking about it. It was changing everything. The search, which had given such specific purpose to his life, or at least to most of his time and activity, was ceasing to exist, and with it were going the demands it had made. The scaffolding was coming down, and it felt as if he were being left with an imaginary building. All it took was information, a picture, a phone number, an address, and he was back at ground level, at the mere idea that started it in the first place. And down there, questions, not answerable by information.

He found Station Street, off the now familiar Township, just above the main highway, a street made invisible by the railway. It had houses only on one side and these had a full view of the railroad yard. The old station had an overhanging roof on all sides and a sign that said FREIGHT. It was shut down for the night. Number 18 was the third house this side of a fork where Station Street divided into a regular street and a gravel service road. He parked in the railroad yard. He saw his hand shaking as he went to open the door. Just that once, it didn't last. He could feel it in his legs. He took a deep breath and got out.

He looked at the big old house, set on a rise, which made it look even bigger, the full gallery, the wide balcony on the second floor, the attic with dormer windows. He glanced at the grounds, full of flowers and bushes, and went up the terraced walk. Some of it needed repair. It felt like somebody's home. And it was. And that excluded him.

On the gallery he rang and waited.

Claudia Poole answered the door. He saw a lively intelligent woman, much like his landlady on Mill Street, with sharp eyes you wouldn't want to lie to. She looked at him without welcome and glanced across the street at the old Dodge.

"Yes?"

"Evening," he said. "Does Adele Symons live here?"

"What makes you think she does?"

"A friend of mine, a lady, phoned you this morning, around ten-thirty."

"Oh, yes. Are you from around here?"

"No."

"Do you know anyone in town?"

"Not really. I know two people to speak of, maybe three, two are out of town."

"Do you want to see her about work?"

"No."

"She's not taking on new work."

"It's not for work."

"What do you want to see her about?"

"It's personal, I used to . . . I'm a friend of hers."

"Oh."

Claudia, sensing something, scrutinized him quickly from head to toe, then hesitated but said nothing more, stepped back a little and pushed the door closed.

He waited. The Dodge looked battered in the low sunlight. Beyond the railroad yard was the highway, the one to East Windsor, the small industries he remembered passing, and beyond that farms, and still farther out more farms, but they only looked like hills. He watched the clouds on the horizon. He had no plan, no stratagem, no tactic. It didn't call for any of that. He felt empty. His legs were still trembling a little. There was a sound at the door and it opened.

Her cheeks were a little less hollow, but it was her. The same auburn hair, recently done up, somewhat paler than he recalled, her eyes a little bluer than gray, the thin nose, her lips a little tighter, chin and jawline perhaps less bony. She seemed more muscular than he remembered. She was wearing a blouse that was more like a shirt, and light rust-colored jeans that had seen a lot of work. She had no makeup. Her eyes were clear, sober, probing. He had no photographs, he'd gone by the memory of her. She was now real. He felt he was about to trespass on something.

"Del," he said, and he could hear the emotion he had tried to keep out of his voice.

She was looking at his eyes to see who knew her, then into them, searched his face, and on hearing his voice, she knew.

"It's you," she said. "Stan."

"Yes."

"You look different."

It was the first thing she noticed, and it made remembering less vivid and delayed the fears that went with it.

He looked at her carefully, to see what his presence might mean, and he thought he saw her face change, first the recognition, the realizing, followed by caution, then fear, most likely.

"How have you been?" he said.

"All right." She let her tone say she wasn't talking about herself. "This is a real surprise. I didn't think I'd ever see you again."

Her frankness cleared away some of the awkwardness. It said the past couldn't be denied. Nor the present.

"Nor did I."

"What are you doing in Ashton?"

"I was looking for you."

"Looking for me?"

She couldn't imagine a reason for such an action, no good reason. It made her suddenly suspicious. It did cross her mind that the door behind her was still open. But somehow she wasn't frightened.

"How did you know I was in Ashton?"

"I didn't. I just kept looking."

"You mean, you were . . . searching for me?"

"Yes."

"Not just in Ashton."

"No. In East Windsor, Middleton."

"That must have taken . . . weeks."

"Months."

"Just to find me?"

"Yes."

"Why, Stan? Why did you want to find me?"

He knew why in his heart, knew it to overflowing, but not in his mind, not as thoughts and reasons that could be stated in so many words. To try to say it, to put it as simple purpose or intent, would be to falsify the whole thing. Still, he had to try.

"Because what happened back then, what I was, and what I did to you, was awful, bad—and I had to acknowledge it for what it was, and know it, and find you, and tell you how sorry I am that it happened. That's why, part of why, I was looking for you."

The past was hurrying back, full of memory and hurt, her hurt, his shame, not nice emotions.

"I'm sorry, too," she said, and by tone and gesture—a look, a hand brushing hair from her brow, body less tense—she indicated that she was going along with what he was saying.

"But sorry doesn't undo it," she said, "it just can't be undone."

"No. It can't. But I couldn't leave it unfaced, and unaccepted, and . . . unsaid, face to face, to you."

"You've really thought it out, haven't you?"

"I'm trying to live it out."

"This . . . realizing . . . when . . . ?"

"In AA, recovering, and after. And since. It's always going on, recovering, I mean."

"I know. You're clean?"

"And dry. Dry-cleaned. We laugh about it in AA."

"I've never laughed about it."

"You say you know. Do you? I mean, did you . . . ?"

"Oh, yes." Her tone suggested the pain of the experience. "I haven't talked about it, outside treatment,

I mean. What I did to—" She stopped herself and looked at him wonderingly. "I can't now. You're something I was getting away from."

He couldn't ask her what she was going to say. It had slipped out like a cry of pain.

"Yes, you had to."

"Face to face is pretty real. It's not like feeling things alone. I mean . . ."

"I know what you mean."

"This kinda churns things up, doesn't it?"

"I'm sorry."

"So much is different now. We're changed, we're . . . strangers."

"Yes."

"Perhaps we always were."

"Could be." Then as he thought of it: "I did find you. I know it's you. That's something."

"Yes. It is, isn't it?"

"Maybe we can talk, just to catch up."

"Not now."

"No. Can I phone you?"

"Yes."

"In a few days?"

"Okay."

He held out his hand and she took it and simply clasped it, no handshake, and let go. Not forgiveness, he didn't expect that, but peace. He knew how rare that is. The moment almost undid him. He made it to the stairs, the walk, the concrete steps, on to the car. Del was still on the gallery.

* * *

He went north on Township, past the hotel, the coin wash, the supermarket, city hall, places he once scrutinized and now no longer saw. Ashton had become a background for Station Street, a place for Del. He knew where she was: he had a street, a number, a house, a phone number, and he'd seen her and talked with her. He marveled at it. The months of not knowing, of looking for that very thing, an address, were nothing compared to the fact of it. They were now the past, already being forgotten. He didn't resent the effort or the discipline, it was part of being sober. He simply dwelt on all this as true, staying in the present, letting go. He had no claims to make, no rights to assert, certainly no rewards to expect. He had never thought that far ahead. There'd been no need till now. And even now there was little he could make happen. He wasn't in charge.

Township Street left town and became the highway to Elizabethville. They'd sprayed calcium on the dirt roads to keep down the dust. The sun was gone, and the greenery was darkening, the air cooling. Kay's red Honda was squeezed over on the lawn to give him room to park. Kay was inside. She had the ball game on the radio, just loud enough to hear.

"You saw her," she said. It wasn't a question.

"I did."

"How about some tea? It's ready."

"Okay."

She kept talking as she poured the tea.

"How is she?"

"She looks fine."

"She must've been surprised."

"Yes, she was."

"She recognize you?"

"Yes, she did. I didn't have to tell her who I was. She had to look, but she knew. Then we talked."

"What's she doing for a living?"

"I didn't ask."

Kay looked at him as if she were trying to keep herself under control. "You mean deliberately?"

"No, I never thought of it. It wasn't the right time for that."

"Well, you were there, you ought to know. How about the child?"

"I didn't see her. We were on the porch. We didn't go inside." Then he almost laughed as he added, "And I didn't ask about her. That's . . . special. And I didn't want to load her with questions. We were talking, that was the main thing."

"Are you being sentimental?"

"No, no. We were meeting, again, like strangers. Not friendly, neutral. Somehow that was important. There'd be plenty of reason not to meet at all. I couldn't blame her. I haven't told you about the past."

"No need. What difference would it make?"

"None at all."

"I can guess it in general. It wouldn't be all that new. You're gonna see her again?"

"I hope to."

"Did you mention me to her?"

"Not yet."

"I'd like to see her. Would that complicate things?"

"There's nothing to complicate. It's up to you."

"I won't butt in."

"That's all right. Thanks for all your help."

"It really wasn't anything, was it?"

"It was something else. It's good to know you."

"You're gonna have me crying."

They laughed. He was glad he'd come.

"I'll be around," he said.

He finished his tea and left.

It was almost fully dark by now. He couldn't go fast on the unlined dirt roads. He got to the other side of Ashton, then to the highway, and on to the gravel roads that led to Martin's. There was no countryside in the distance, in fact no distance, no landmarks to go by, only abstract yellow signs about what lay five hundred feet ahead.

At Martin's the yard lights were on, big bright floods that backlit the maples along the driveway and made him feel he was driving into a movie. He parked just past the sheds not to obstruct anything, he knew his way around. It felt, just for an instant, like getting home.

Martin was in the kitchen. Stan knew he'd waited up.

"How'd it go?"

"I found her."

It evoked time and meaning and suggested the feelings just behind the words. Stan made some instant coffee and told him about it, simply, without analyzing anything. Finding Del was something he was still gawking at. Like Ashton, Martin's was beginning to be different. His reason for being there had changed. And he could sense himself, inside, shifting with the events, becoming a little afraid. A signal for a drink. He had the coffee.

"It was good to see her. The way she was, was good. I even imagined she was glad to see me. That's naïve, isn't it?"

"Just human. Kids feel that way. They feel so good about you they make you feel good. It works."

"They haven't got a past. The past always feels like a mistake, doesn't it?"

"Most of the time it is. That's one of the things you carry around. Like your self."

"A couple of selves and you've got a lot of luggage."

"Depends. Don't let it get you down, you know better."

"Yeah. People seem to create one another, don't they? I mean, they seem to make each other grow, bent or otherwise."

"It's we, not they. We do that. With a blessing or a curse, very old. So old we think it's not there."

"It's there. God, but it's there."

7

❦

He thought about it all day, and by evening he felt there was no point in waiting. He dialed the Station Street number. It was near eight. He got Mrs. Poole.

"Hello. Can I speak to Del, please?"

"Who's calling?"

"Stan Hagan."

"Is she expecting your call?"

"In a general way, yes."

"Just a minute."

There were muffled voices and Del came on. "Hello, Stan."

Her voice sounded clear and resonant. He couldn't recall ever having phoned her. It seemed to say something about the past.

"Del. I know it's soon, but I wanted to call."

"That's all right. It's not that soon anymore."

"Can we meet? I'd like to see you."

"I don't know."

"Just to talk, to catch up on things."

"That's not going to make much difference."

"It doesn't have to make any difference."

"I'd have to make the time. That'd make it seem important."

"It doesn't have to seem important, a time to talk, anytime. It's not a date."

"No, it's not. It's just that I can't afford any upsets. I have too much to keep going."

"There won't be any upsets. I won't turn up without being invited. Yesterday was just that once."

"I thought as much, but I didn't know."

"I don't want to intrude on your life. I can ask, that's all. If you say no, it's no."

"Why do you want this, Stan? What's your purpose?"

"I have no purpose. I mean, no plans or anything like that." And as if to explain he added, "I've been thinking about you for months and I'd like to see you."

He said it plainly, without calculation. Del didn't say anything for a while.

"All right," she finally said. "How about Saturday? In the afternoon."

"That's fine. At Station Street?"

"Yes."

Martin decided to try it alone. It wasn't much of a decision, there was no other way. Stan wouldn't be staying on much longer, he knew, and things would return to normal. That meant the quiet, now slower, routines of solitude, taking the long times that working alone takes. It had been a good two weeks. And they were over. You don't hold on. He was fine. He'd driven to Sherbrooke on Thursday, the rainy day he'd waited for, and gone to the hospital clinic. Nothing turned up on the machines. The young doctor said he was doing well, considering. He had wanted to ask him how he knew, what he got from the apparatus that made him so sure, but he said nothing, it would be unfair, a sudden plunge into another kind of thinking, and he let the comedy stay, unremarked.

He moved the tractor from its own shed and backed it to the end of that row of buildings. He left the motor running, got off slowly, and at the shed he removed the padlock, hung it on the open hasp, and after an initial effort to get it moving he pushed the big door open along its track. He was aware of all the moves he was making. Inside he went to a flatbed trailer, swung down its hitching arm, and laid it on a block of wood. The trailer was a six-by-sixteen four-wheeler made of three-by-twelve planking, open on the long sides and stopped at the ends with four-by-four posts. He checked the tires, the planks, the posts, and got back on the tractor and lined it up, hitch to hitch, locked the brakes, got off again, and dropped in the hitch pin and secured it. His decision had him working again. It was after lunch on Saturday. Stan was getting ready to bring the laundry to town, and to see Del. It was dry weather, a good time to haul firewood from the bush.

He moved the rig out and turned it into the open

field toward the woods. He followed a worn-down trail and set the gears and throttle to let the rig heave and not bounce over the rough spots. All he had to do was steer. The hay on all sides looked long enough to cut. There was no wind. In a week the weeds would begin to show in the garden, things grew fast this time of year, mid-June, and he'd have to look after it. It was just a matter of walking through the paths with the tiller. Simple. It was hot out in the open. He stood up to take off his denim jacket and flipped it onto the flatbed. It looked funny there, it reminded him of youngsters leaving their clothes anywhere. So long ago. Yet still with him. Clear, sudden, not memory exactly, more like the return of presences. No mistake about that past. That came later. He watched the advancing bush. It would be cool in there.

When he was within sight of the mounds of chopped wood, he circled left among the trees and made a wide U-turn and placed the rig between two piles of wood, pointing home. It was planned that way from the start, it made it easier to load and easier to get out. He had learned it the first time he ever tried it, by getting stuck, unloading, still stuck, getting help, much to the sustained amusement of Phil Baines, his new neighbor then, and the men he'd brought with him. How easily they worked, and how intelligently. Years of experience, years. He put on his jacket as a wry concession to aging muscles, and looked at the silent woods. That, too, was part of being there.

The flatbed was about waist high and could hold four rows of corded wood. He began by laying out pieces down the middle of the wagon until he had the beginning of two inside rows. It took time, sixteen feet is a lot of feet, twice, once from each side. He always thought of the local adage, which was probably universal, and always laughed: Wood warms you twice, once when you chop it, and once when you burn it. It wasn't true enough, it warmed you every time you went near it. When he felt up to it, he started building up the row on his side. It was work that couldn't be hurried, one piece at a time, from pile to wagon, laid snugly in place, the row kept vertical, no leaning, it would be braced later by the second row. He took to doing a few pieces and stopping. He didn't plan to do much, only as high as he could easily reach. Even then it wasn't light work, five pounds and more at the end of your arm, only habit and knowledge made it seem easy. The fact of it was different.

He didn't realize how long he'd been at it. He was stopping more than he was working. He decided to take a long break. He took off his jacket and walked it over to the tractor like a man wasting time, and draped it over the seat. He was tiring, a little too soon, he felt, but he could hardly avoid knowing it. He sat on one of the chopping blocks and rested, but the fatigue remained. The pile hadn't gone down much, it never seems to until you're almost finished. The row on the wagon, though long, was only two and three pieces high. It looked meager in all that space. He'd wanted to see how much he could do alone, to plan from there, to do, not what had to be done, but what could be done. He was finding out. It mightn't be much after all. At this rate it would take twenty trips. A month maybe, if it didn't rain too much. He sat for a long time, knowing what it all meant, and tried it again.

But not for long. There was a subtle change of tone to everything. The piles of wood took on the look of something that wouldn't get done. The tractor and the flatbed seemed huge and ponderous, out of place somehow for being outside, not stored, at home. The pieces were getting too heavy. He stopped. It was enough. The site, cleared for passage, strewn with work a team of men might have done, began to feel deserted, as if one man, there, alone, could only be a spectator. Finding out takes a little time; deciding, a little longer. He had to give up, but he didn't want to give in. Subtle. He couldn't think it out. Accept it. Something's there.

He climbed aboard the tractor, with effort, the jacket still on the seat, and started it, and got it going, third gear low, not pulling much of a load. Accept it for what it is, this is as much as you're going to do. The subtle change ran deep, and it had him wondering. The ride back seemed long and slow.

He stopped the rig outside the woodshed and simply got off. His one thought was to get into the house and lie down. Something was happening. He made it to the kitchen, sat for a moment, and surer now, and weaker, he went to the chair by the phone and, laboriously, hoping he wouldn't forget as he went along, he dialed the Baineses' number. He held on as it rang and rang. Marge answered.

"It's me, Martin, I'm going to need help."

It was all he could get out. He managed to hang up.

He got himself to the floor and, quite sure now, accepting, he lost consciousness.

Stan made a wide turn in the station's lot and pulled up in front of the Poole house. He'd phoned ahead from the booth near the coin wash. There'd been lots of people and one of the dryers wasn't working. He tried not to hurry, then not to feel hurried, but it was no good. He wanted to get to Station Street. He rang and waited. Just arriving and ringing and waiting felt like an accomplishment. As if it was too good to be true. He was surprised at his feelings. They presumed an innocence he didn't have.

Del answered the door, looked at him straight in the eyes, "Hello, Stan," and stepped out on the porch. She was in a blouse and skirt and flat shoes. She had a large purse slung over her right shoulder.

"Del."

It was clear they weren't going inside. He hadn't expected to.

"This is not my house," she said, as if to explain it.

"That's all right."

She moved toward the stairs, and they began walking down to the street.

"Mrs. Poole likes to fuss over me. She's worried about this."

"And you?"

"I am, too."

There was nothing he could say to reassure her, it would only be words, the same words that lies would use.

They crossed to the railroad station. There was no traffic. They walked on the paved platform.

"She doesn't want you moving in."

She said it calmly, but firmly, stating her own resistance to something he might be taking for granted. He almost laughed at the frankness of it, but a tone in her voice precluded it.

"I wasn't thinking of it."

"I can't know that."

"No, you can't. Not till it's not done. Only time would tell you that."

She gave him a long look. He sounded as if he'd thought about things a lot.

"All right."

He understood her to mean that it wasn't worth arguing over, that it was something that simply had to be brought up.

"I'd like to hear about you," he said, "how you made out."

"No. I'm not there yet, Stan, it would be asking too much."

"Sure."

"Tell me about yourself."

He realized she had to know. He didn't want to hurt her all over again, so he began with his hitting bottom and calling AA. He told her of his struggles to attain sobriety, the suggested steps of the program, his resolve to find her and make amends, the long search that followed. He told her about Kay Saunders and Martin Lacey. He didn't mention the baby, he felt he should wait for a proper moment.

"Kay saw the picture in the paper. That's how I found you."

"How is Kay?"

"She's fine."

"I didn't go back. I should have, she was good to me. I was really down. Then I didn't, I simply didn't."

"Del," he said, and groped for the next words. She looked at him. "Del, Kay told me everything she knew."

"The baby."

"Yes. You haven't mentioned her."

"I didn't know if you'd resent her."

"Resent her? Oh, God. Perhaps then. Yeah, you're right. But not now. She's been on my mind ever since I heard."

There was tense silence for a long while.

"There's more," Del said.

"What?"

"She was born addicted. My addiction." Del couldn't go on. Her eyes were running tears.

"If she ever goes near drugs"—she managed to make her words clear—"she'll be an addict right off. It's waiting for her. I'll have to explain when the time comes. I hope she believes me."

She began walking across the street to the house.

"Del."

"Yes."

"Can I see her?"

She nodded yes.

He waited on the gallery. He could almost count his feelings as they surfaced, guilt and sorrow and resentment and fear. And something that wouldn't let go, something he didn't dare call love. He let them be. When Del appeared, she had Betty in her arms. The child was still a little sleepy. She was in a yellow jumper, worn at the knees with crawling.

"This is Betty," Del said.

Stan put his hand on the child's head and felt the warmth. He didn't say anything.

"Maybe she'll go to you. She just got up."

Del held the child out to Stan. "She's usually good with strangers."

He took Betty, who didn't mind, and kept looking at her, no baby talk, no phony cheerfulness.

"How old is she?"

"Fourteen months. She's about ready to start walking."

It took him back over what had been a long time.

"She was a month early."

He nodded at what Del said and stared at the child. Finally he grinned at her and she responded and said something in syllables.

Del said, "She wants her bear."

Stan laughed a little at the interpretation. And he gently handed Betty to Del.

"I'll take her in, she's used to her toys when she wakes up."

Again he waited, aware, almost bitterly, of the isolation each of them was in, the distance to cover. It seemed impossible.

When Del came back, he led the way down the steps to the first landing of the terrace. They stood there in silence looking out over the highway and the countryside.

When he felt he was ready, he turned to Del and said: "She's also mine, isn't she?"

"Yes, she is."

And then, to be sure, beyond all metaphor, even sentiment: "I'm her father."

"Yes."

He felt as though a reality had been bestowed on him, something unchangeable. It was a long way from a nothingness he remembered.

Softly he grasped her shoulder, once, to be in touch. "Can I phone you?"

"Yes."

He drove slowly to the corner. He stopped and waited and almost forgot what he'd stopped for. There was no traffic and hardly any people. He turned south on Township. It had become a warm dusty Saturday afternoon. He made a point of noticing it, just to keep his own head from getting too busy. It felt late, 4:39 when he looked. He took a right at Main, going west. She was fourteen months old. That meant—when he got past his own resistance and counted back—that meant nothing good about him.

After a few blocks he went very slowly past the cars parked outside the church. The pickup wasn't there. It wasn't on the side street, and it wasn't in the back parking lot. He parked on Main and went inside.

He looked carefully for Martin and didn't see him. The priest was offering the bread and wine. He sat at the very back trying to heed the words at the altar, but again and again he found himself looking the people over systematically. It was too late for Martin to be merely late. He probably stayed in the bush too long, he didn't wear a watch when he worked. He had hoped to see him there and to sit with him this time.

He'd be moving out now, of course, and getting a job, a real job. Whatever else happened, he couldn't walk away from the child. They'd had a life, a complexity of daily living, without him, and he his, each with its own kind of suffering. How difficult to get back to the human. He couldn't get over it. How distant belief was. Distracted as he was, he turned to it, glad there was something physical, a tangible simplicity, bread. I ask as I am, it can't be otherwise. It was a new kind of emptiness, full of people he wanted to be with.

Outside, he waited till the cars left, just to be sure. Then he drove with purpose along Main, going east, and out of town. On the dirt road he made a lot of dust. He slowed down, not to overtax the air filter, but found that too slow. He wanted to find out about Martin, and that couldn't be done slowly. To hell with the filter. He skidded on the turns and kept ahead of the mountains of dust he was making. With the fast driving his feelings started to run high. He forced himself to slow down, to let the car do the work, to let easy do it. It took effort. At the mailbox he stopped and turned carefully into the driveway.

The pickup was in front of the main porch, out of the way, where he'd last seen it. Things were quiet, empty. He saw the tractor, the flatbed, the long low rows of corded wood. He took the two laundry bags from the wagon. He assumed Martin was inside. He went over to the tractor. He saw the jacket pressed down on the seat, the key in the ignition, the work that had stopped.

The kitchen door was locked. He'd gone out, somebody had given him a lift. He didn't quite believe that. It took him a moment to remember the key under the roof. A bird's nest. He felt cold. He put the bags down, opened the door, put the key back, and carried the bags in.

Inside there was only silence.

"Mr. Lacey."

He didn't expect a greeting. The chair wasn't by the phone where it usually was. He looked into Martin's bedroom. Nothing. Then all the other rooms, the front porch, the basement. On a sudden thought, he checked the sheds. Still nothing. He brought in the jacket and the tractor key.

He sat at the kitchen table, trying to organize his thoughts, to plan how to find out what was going on.

"His friends."

Near the phone he found a well-worn alphabetic booklet and tried to think of the name of the people Martin had mentioned. I don't know anything about him, just him. Isn't that—? The phone rang.

Martin's ring or not, he didn't wait, he picked it up.

"Yes."

"You're Stan?"

"Yes, yes."

"I'm Marge Baines, I saw you go by, with that car and all the dust, so I—"

"Is it about Mr. Lacey?"

"Yes."

"Something happened."

"Yes, it did. They took him to the hospital."

"Where?"

"In Sherbrooke. My husband went with him."

"How do I find it?"

She told him.

It took about forty minutes to get to the city, a few more to find the hospital, park, and look for a likely entrance. He went in where it said EMERGENCY. A dozen or so people sat on long benches in the lobby and near doors that had signs for this and that. Four or five children were doing what children do, on the move, at a water fountain, a soft-drink machine. The desk took up one side of the lobby. There was no one there. Nurses moved in and out of doors along the corridor. The place looked busy and tedious, both. He decided to wait at the desk, hoping things wouldn't get too complicated when he started asking questions. He'd stopped hurrying. They were the ones who could do something, not him. And then as he looked around, it got very simple.

There was a pay phone on the other side of the lobby. Using it was a big man around sixty, in work clothes, with short gray hair, a farmer by the look of him. Stan crossed the lobby and stood about ten feet from him. The big man caught Stan's eye and held up a hand just-a-minute. His eyes were wet. When he hung up, he came over.

"I take it you're Stan. I'm Phil Baines. I was just telling my wife."

"She called me at Mr. Lacey's. How's he doing?"

"Martin's dead."

Stan was silent. He felt his face move as if he were chewing something. His eyes stung.

The big man sighed. "Sorry I didn't get to meet you," he said. "He liked you, liked the way you worked."

He could feel the man's sorrow, his reticence, a long-time friend. Martin somehow had made things real. It made a difference.

"He gave me a lot," Stan said. "More than he realized."

"Yeah. He was like that." Then: "Marge and I will be looking after things. I've already told them. Can you give me a ride back?"

"Sure. In a minute. I want to do something."

"All right. I'll be here."

At the desk he said to a woman in a white smock: "I'd like to see Mr. Lacey."

"Are you a relative?"

"No."

"Oh. You can't. You see . . ."

"I know that. I want to see him anyway."

"We usually don't allow that."

"I want to see him."

He held her eye. She was human. She got up without a word and led him to an elevator, then to the basement, along one corridor, another, and through a door marked AUTOPSY.

"Wait here."

She went through a wide door that opened automatically. He was in some sort of anteroom. There was nothing in it, just light and the air grilles. As he wondered about that, she came through the automatic door pushing a wheeled table. From the form on it she pulled back the covering partway and stepped aside without seeming to move.

Stan looked at Martin's face. A lot had gone with this man. And a lot had stayed.

"I'll ask, Mr. Lacey. I'll keep asking."

He turned to the woman, thinking she'd wheel the table away. But she just nodded and led him back upstairs.

"Thank you."

"That's all right."

He left with Phil Baines.

He turned down Phil's offer of supper and went to Martin's to do a few last things. He locked the sheds, the pickup, put the keys on the kitchen table. He couldn't leave abruptly, just like that. He felt something had to be acknowledged. He took time to eat, remembering, trying not to grieve at the very real silence, but weeping softly anyway and doing nothing to stop it. It was a response to the real. He cleaned up after him, then around the house, made sure all the windows were closed. He got his things, locked up, and put them in the wagon. He looked for a while at the garden. Then he left and drove to Ashton. He went back to the Mill Street rooms and made a deal with the landlady; he was nearly out of money. And later that evening he rode around and got to Kay's to give her the news.

The next day he went to the wake early, when he thought no one would be around. But there were quite a few people, no one he recognized. He went simply because it wasn't over yet. He spoke to no one, he felt he had no title, he wasn't family, or a known friend, just a sort of hired hand who wouldn't be noticed or missed. It seemed to fit in with Martin's quiet way. It made him wonder about how we know each other. Later he phoned Del, it was too soon for him to go over, and told her what was going on.

The following morning he attended the funeral. He sat at the back, in the same church, watching it come to an end. The woman his age he took to be Martin's daughter, the man his son, the others relatives and friends. He saw the Baineses, and the man from the hardware store. When it was over, he stayed to watch the line of cars go slowly down Main Street and turn out of sight.

From there he went to Station Street. He'd been invited this time, which made things seem more normal. Del answered the door.

"You can come in," she said.

"Thanks. But I'd rather not."

He didn't feel like being scrutinized by Mrs. Poole.

"Just for coffee."

"No, thanks. I'd like to ask you something else."

"What is it?"

"What do you say we go visit Kay Saunders?"

Del thought it over and decided.

"All right. I'll get Betty."

It was something they could do together. He went to the wagon and stood by it, waiting. He'd remembered, and asked. It was going to be a different kind of day-to-day living. Easy would have to do that too.